THE DSA SEASON ONE, BOOK TWO

PROMETHEAN

Also by Lou Paduano

The Greystone Saga

Signs of Portents
Tales from Portents
The Medusa Coin
Pathways in the Dark
A Circle of Shadows

Greystone-in-Training

Hammer and Anvil

The DSA

Season One
The Clearing

THE DSA SEASON ONE, BOOK TWO

PROMETHEAN

Lou Paduano

Eleven Ten Publishing LLC

GRAND ISLAND, NEW YORK

Eleven Ten Publishing LLC
282 Fareway Lane
Grand Island, NY 14072

Publisher's note: This is a work of fiction. Names, characters, places, and incidents either are the product of the author's imagination or are used fictitiously. Any resemblance to actual events, locales, or persons, living or dead, is entirely coincidental.

Printed in the United States of America
Edited by JD Book Services.
Cover art design by MiblArt

First edition published 2019

Library of Congress Cataloguing in Publication Data
Paduano, Lou
Promethean / Lou Paduano

LCCN: 2019914390
ISBN-13: 978-1-944965-19-8 (paperback)
ISBN-13: 978-1-944965-18-1 (eBook)

CHAPTER ONE

Fingers clutched tightly to the envelope in Henry Reed's hand. They grazed the seal decorating the back, which was an image of a man resting under an apple tree with a single object falling from the branches above.

He didn't open it—the instructions had been clear. The package had arrived while his mother rested in her room. The treatments had taken their toll on her and her exhaustion stretched longer with each visit to the doctor. Her name was noted on the label. This was her task, but he refused to disturb her slumber. She was sick and needed him, the way he had always needed her.

It was time to return the favor.

Beyond the lone envelope in the shallow box was a handwritten note. Sparse language described the situation, little in the way of details offered besides the time and location.

SHUR-RITE BUILDING
REGINALD KANE
NOW

Downtown Chicago stretched out before him. The drive was lost to the note and the circumstances of the package's arrival. How often had these deliveries occurred? Had he failed to notice all these years or had his mother hidden them from him? The questions carried him to the Shur-Rite facility. It towered over him and he stood in its shadow for a long moment. The December chill cut through him. He failed to feel it, heat rising along his skin.

Extravagant fixtures showered light from the walls of the extensive lobby. They guided visitors through the revolving door to the waiting security guard within. Henry took the slow walk, swallowing his nerves with each step.

"Courier?" the guard asked upon arriving.

"Yeah," Henry mumbled, hand to the back of his neck. He lifted the letter for the man to see, evidence of his intention. "I'm here to see Reginald Kane."

The guard passed along a sign-in sheet and dropped a pen on top. Henry picked up the instrument, then he paused. He didn't want his mother in trouble for him taking over her delivery. Using the seal along the back of the envelope as inspiration, Henry played it safe. He scribbled the first name that came to mind.

"Here a little late today," the guard said. He placed the clipboard aside without looking, the routine of the event clearly mundane to his day.

"Request just came in," Henry said with a disarming smile, while his stomach managed a triple somersault.

"Mr. Kane and his snail mail," said the guard, shaking his head.

"Some people don't like change."

The guard laughed. He led Henry to the elevator bank at the end of the hall. He inserted his key and the car in the center opened.

"Ain't that the truth," he said. "Test drove a new truck the other day and the thing starts blaring like I hit the self-destruct button. They have some new warning about leaving something in the backseat. I damn well thought there was a ghost back there instead of just my jacket."

Henry smiled as he slipped inside the waiting elevator. "I guess some people don't like surprises either."

"Smart kid," the guard said with a tip of his hat. "I'll let Mr. Kane know you're on your way."

"Thank you."

The door closed and Henry settled along the back of the rising car. His heart slowed, falling once again into a natural rhythm. Why he was so nervous he had no idea. The delivery of a letter was a simple task. Yet everything about the situation appeared strange to the young man. He was out of his element. He had struggled to make ends meet to take care of his mother's growing hospital bills. The money at the base of the package helped at a desperate time. He couldn't risk losing it now.

He arrived at the seventh floor of the Shur-Rite Building without pomp and pageantry. Nothing but darkness lined the hall, offices stretching on both sides. The only light at that late hour beamed from the far end and the lone open door.

Henry took a breath, letter squeezed along his side. He inched down the corridor, where the sound of shouting amplified with each step toward the occupied office.

"I understand the issue," the voice boomed. A shadow ran along the door, causing Henry to shrink back. A man with a phone to his ear paced the vast space. "I've been doing this a long time. No, that wasn't a comment on your youth, you idiot. When things go wrong, you should learn to take a damn breath before finding someone to blame. The trucks *will* be found. Whoever diverted them from our South Bend facility will be dealt with. It will be handled. No, I shuttered the operation as a contingency. There are no loose ends to find there."

Henry stopped outside the office. The name Reginald Kane decorated the door, the title of Chief Operating Officer underneath. Kane stood tall, a drink in his left hand and a phone in his right. His salt-and-pepper hair was perfectly placed, and his suit was snug against his wiry frame.

"An explanation?" Kane exclaimed, nearly spilling his drink. He finished it and slammed the glass against the mantel before resuming his trek through the office. "I was out of the country, you smug piece of... Listen to me. I have responsibilities outside of the group. We all do. But I have been in this for decades. I know the importance of what has happened, and the study we could have accomplished with the Spring Hill incident. I wasn't the one who insisted on incinerating the rest of the specimens. No... I have never seen this nut with the glasses before, but if you think that means you can pin this at my doorstep, you can forget it."

Kane circled his desk. He stopped at the intercom near the edge. A red light flashed and the man's eyes snapped toward the door and his waiting visitor.

"Find the drivers," Kane barked into the phone. "Find *something*. Then you can scream at me."

The phone clicked and he dropped the device upon the chair

on his way to the door. He pulled it open and Henry stood, an awkward and nervous look on his face.

"What the hell is this now?"

"Sorry to interr—"

"Shut it," Kane snapped. He returned to the mantel and poured a new drink. "How long have you been at the door?"

"I just—"

"Speak up."

Henry entered the office warily. He extended the letter. "I was asked to deliver this."

Kane snatched the envelope from the young man even as he winced at the burning liquor slipping down his throat. He lowered the glass. His eyes widened at sight of the seal on the back.

"I wasn't expecting anything," Kane said. "And you're not my usual courier."

Henry stayed quiet, unsure what to say. Kane returned to his desk, where he opened the top drawer. His hand hovered over the contents within the deep nook then removed a letter opener. After tearing through the thin paper, Kane retrieved the note.

"What the hell is this? Some kind of joke?"

"I don't—"

Kane flipped the paper around. It contained one word.

GOODBYE

"You think this is funny?" Kane yelled. He tore the letter, dropping the pieces into the waiting trash. "Who the hell are you?"

"I have no—"

Kane reached into the drawer once again. He snatched a metallic device from inside, and immediately leveled it at Henry. A revolver.

"Who are you?" he repeated.

"H… Henry," the young man stammered. He backed away, blocked by the various furniture spread throughout the office. He kept his hands open and wide. Terror caused him to sweat. "Please, I don't—"

"First Weingard pulls this crap on the phone and now *this*?" Kane seethed. "Those damn trucks."

"Listen," Henry pleaded. "I delivered whatever it was I was

supposed to deliver, so I'd like to—"

"What?" Kane said. "What would you like, Henry? You know what I would like?"

Henry tripped over the leg of the chair and fell to the floor. He rolled with the impact, then worked his way to his knees. The gun was waiting for him, inches from his scalp.

"Two decades in this endeavor," Kane continued. "I have made the Trust more money than anyone. And this is it? Some fluke mistake and they send you? Not going to happen."

"Listen. Please, listen. I don't know what you think this is, but—"

"I know exactly what this is," Kane said, a wry smirk forming. He cocked the hammer back on his weapon. "And here's my rebuttal. Make sure they get the message."

Heat surged through his chest. "Please—"

"Begging?" Kane condemned. "Man up, Henry."

The young man closed his eyes. "I wasn't…"

The gun pressed tight to his forehead. "Enough with the mumbling!"

"Please, I…" Henry took a long breath. It did little to stem the heat coursing through his terrified body. He reached up and grabbed the man's arm. The heat grew along with the terrified eyes of Henry Reed. "I wasn't begging for me."

"What?" Kane staggered back. Flames sparked up his sleeve. He dropped the revolver, and the weapon discharged violently when it hit the floor. The crack of the gun forced Henry to the ground to avoid the bullet as it slammed into the mantel behind him. "It can't be…"

The flames engulfed Kane's torso. Screams of pain echoed along the seventh floor. The panicked executive collapsed on the carpet. The fire spread down his legs. The terror in his eyes was lost to the flames.

"No, I didn't mean to…" Henry reached for him, far too late to do any good.

"*Promethean…*" Kane muttered. His skin bubbled, his body breaking down from the intense heat consuming him.

"Oh, God." Henry stared deep into the flames as Kane met his end. Tears streamed along his cheeks. "I'm sorry. I'm so sorry."

CHAPTER TWO

Ben Riley raced along Greentree Road toward Ashburton. The digital clock over the neighborhood pharmacy inched toward ten in the morning. The snow in the greater Bethesda area had departed earlier in the week, bringing a warm front and unusually mild mornings. Still, mid-to-high thirties made for a somewhat frigid jog. The wind was just the cherry on top as far as Ben was concerned, smiling and waving at a group of power walkers before making the turn to Fernwood.

He'd taken the same route all week—an early-morning bus trip from his apartment to a stop on Bradmoor. From there, he started his trek north, taking the bridge over the Beltway. A number of residential neighborhoods offered a distraction from the bitter temperatures. The beautiful homes marking the sides of the trail also gave Ben something else, something much needed during his jog.

Windows.

Large picture windows dotted the homes that stretched along Inglemere and Greyswood. They allowed him tiny glances at the passing traffic, while he toyed with his shoelaces. Ben counted the seconds, his breath wafting against the cold. Five seconds and then he saw it.

The gray sedan.

Blacked-out windows, no visible plates, and the quick turn after passing made it clear that they were not in the area for the scenery.

The same occurred on Fernwood. He allowed a short pause in front of a coffee shop, this time under the guise of an untied sneaker. The day before, it had been to stretch while waiting for the light at the corner to change in his favor. A count of five and another sedan, this one lighter in color but carrying the same blacked-out windows. Not wanting to draw unnecessary attention, he smiled politely to a woman exiting the cafe, finished fiddling with his red-and-white-striped sneakers, and started north once more.

Ben continued along Fernwood toward the Westfield Montgomery Mall. A black sedan picked up where their companion left off. He noted the change as the door closed and he entered the food court.

"Thanks," Ben replied with a smile, beaming at the mango peach smoothie handed his way. The woman behind the counter offered a wide grin with his purchase. Over the course of the week Ben had discovered how truly personable his new friend Tamara — definitely not Tammy or Mara — was, learning about her current enrollment at a community college before she hoped to make the leap to a four-year school out of state and away from her overprotective and dismally boring parents. Communications, whatever that actually meant, was her major, though she liked to focus in what she labeled as *more interesting* areas. Ben fought back all follow-up questions to the twenty-year-old brunette, keeping his responses firmly on the smoothie business.

It was a tough fight to win.

Beverage in hand, Ben found a table waiting for him in the center of the bustling food court. Around him, people swarmed the mall in a ravenous spree that could only mean the holidays were in full swing.

December had snuck up on him. As a kid it had always been a time for family. As an adult it became a time of laughter and companionship. The loss of his former life in Buffalo, where he'd been framed for crimes he never committed, left him with no friends and no family. Suffice it to say, he found the holidays to be less than a priority. Not that he needed another one.

Since Bellbrook, his nights had been spent dreaming of his last moments with Ruth Heller, the lead field agent in his unit at the Department of Special Assignments. He had done everything in his power to save her yet could not help but feel guilty for her passing. The blame, however, lay with another face from his nightmares.

The Witness.

"I am not your enemy. When this ends, when all this finally ends, I will be your only hope for survival. Remember that, Benjamin Riley."

The man's last words echoed in Ben's brain like a catchy pop song on repeat. He had known about Ben. He had known about Ben's recruitment to the DSA. All of which had taken place mere days before the Bellbrook incident. Most of the department still had not learned his name. The Witness had known that and more.

"There is a reason you are here. A reason you have been chosen by them..."

Ben blew off the claim. He refused to believe there was anything behind it except the hope for self-doubt and fear in the small clearing outside Bellbrook, Ohio. He refused to carry any notion that the move to the DSA was anything more than what it was.

The three men that followed him into the mall made Ben reconsider.

Never standing together, yet always within view of the others, each one used a different door. They surrounded the food court and took up positions throughout the area. One sat at a table with a newspaper and a cup of coffee, which were conspicuously not from one of the shops in the mall. Another stood near the condiments outside the Charley's eatery, without any food or tray in sight. The third stretched lightly, pretending to gear up for some heavy-duty mall walking.

There were others. The obvious couple that seemed overly jovial, making their conversation heard when they passed by, yet never saying a word after they sat on the other side of the court. The impromptu business meeting that never made it past the introductions, and always kept Ben in sight. The faces changed daily, but the gimmicks continued.

Ben had to smile at the effort. For all their work—and it was top-notch surveillance—they simply forgot who they were monitoring. He made the surveillance as easily as the sedans outside. Earpieces just out of view. Staggered glances in his direction. Even with the Christmas rush they stood out to the former beat cop. In truth, however, they might have had a fighting chance against him had his internal alert status not been at a standing red.

Had he not found the bugs in his apartment.

His DSA-appointed apartment.

Discovering the first had been strictly an accident. A broken lamp in the fully furnished two-bedroom unit displayed the device in all its glory. The eleven that followed had taken the rest of the day to locate. It wasn't a stretch to see the lengths someone was willing to go to keep tabs on him. The jogging in December certainly made that clear. And calling them *someone* wasn't exactly accurate. He knew who the bugs belonged to.

He just didn't know why.

The morning food-court ritual with Tamara and the mango peach smoothie of his dreams had begun as a ploy to draw out any other surveillance. Ben, however, saw it as something more when he viewed the onslaught of shoppers amid those labeled as regulars.

It was an opportunity.

Mall walkers roamed the halls. Older couples did their daily regimented exercises. Shopaholics, if that was still something to be called, visited daily. Parents with strollers tried to escape the confines of their homes during the winter months. All were routinely visible throughout the mall — like clockwork.

Ben had spent the week watching them just as clearly as he was being watched by the surveillance team that swarmed the food court. He waited for an opening: an opportunity to get in touch with someone that could help shed some light on his current situation. He needed to contact someone outside his current life with the DSA — someone he could trust.

A young mother carted her navy-blue stroller toward the restrooms, the same act he'd witnessed to the minute over the last three days. Ben started to stand to follow. As his foot hit the tiled floor, he stopped.

His phone was ringing in his pocket.

Head slumping, Ben sat back at the table in the food court. His chance faded down the restroom corridor. The phone continued to ring incessantly as his hand struggled to release it from his pocket. The delay caused an older woman at an adjacent table to throw a dirty look for interrupting her morning fiber intake.

Ben accepted the call. He kept his eyes low and away from both the curious stares of his neighbor and the individuals being paid to glare at him.

"Leave a message after the beep," he chimed. "BEEEEEEEEEP."

"Where are you?" the whine of Zac Modine's voice buzzed in his ear.

Ben pulled the phone away and lowered the volume, while reaching for his smoothie. He took a long, drawn-out sip. It echoed into the receiver. Smacking his lips, he let the cup hit the surface of the table before bringing the phone back to his ear.

"At home watching cartoons. Want to ask what I'm wearing?" The older woman's eyes bulged at the question. Ben smiled. He covered the phone's speaker, leaning toward the busybody. "It's my mom. We have a loving relationship."

The woman huffed and immediately left. Ben chuckled, happy to call it a win for privacy.

The Head of Operational Support and Research coughed into the line. "Finish your shopping and head to the airport."

"How did you—?" Ben fought to keep his eyes on the smoothie and away from the men and women circling his position. He flitted between them, curious to their reaction. Was Zac involved in his surveillance?

"GPS on your phone," Zac answered. "Nothing magical."

Ben tapped the table, beads of sweat forming on his forehead. "You take away the sense of wonder, Modine."

"I'm sure you'll always be a Toys R Us kid, Riley. Flight for Chicago leaves in two hours."

The phone clicked before Ben could reply. He let the warm device sit in his hands for a long moment, then stood. The woman with the stroller was already on her way back down the long corridor of the mall. Ben checked his watch, his opportunity shot for the day.

The DSA, the organization following him, needed him again. It was another case without a soul to rely on—without one person to trust. He lifted his smoothie cup and drained it with a long, satisfied sip. "Peachy."

CHAPTER THREE

Morgan Dunleavy waited for the call to end. She paced through the seventh-floor office of Reginald Kane. She tried not to listen, hoping the response would be favorable—knowing it wouldn't be.

"Riley's on his way," Zac said from the hall. He refused to enter the crime scene, where the smell had immediately sent him reeling for the restroom near the elevators. As long as he kept his eyes locked on her and never on the surrounding area, the out-of-his-element tech appeared stable. Or as stable as Zac could be given his current assignment.

Morgan nodded without a glance in his direction. She circled the large black dot eclipsing the pristine carpet of the office: the very spot where Kane's remains had been found mere hours earlier by security.

Local authorities still held jurisdiction, though that would change when the FBI arrived. Kane's murder had made the morning news, and the pissing contest to see who would get the glory for solving the case was going to be more engrossing than anything gleaned from the victim.

Morgan fought for access, the field office for the Bureau giving the DSA a chance to close the case before more bodies hit the floor. Or burned to death, as was the situation at Shur-Rite.

There were no clear markings on the rug other than the lone circle, almost like a campfire had been set up in the center of the office building. Controlled and contained. Fire didn't work that way, not out in the open. And not with the damage found on Kane's body.

Closing the case slipped further away with each question

raised. Still, Morgan shot back at her colleague in irritation. "I didn't ask you to call him."

Zac turned, his eyes wandering toward the ceiling. "I was following procedure."

"I can handle this," Morgan reiterated. The words sounded better, almost confident, especially compared to the pit growing in her stomach over the case. Kane's death made no sense in the conventional sense. There was no ignition source from the blaze that had cooked him alive. The only residue captured for evidence came from a missing firearm, the .45 caliber slug embedded in the wall next to the mantel.

"Lincoln wasn't available?"

"He's been pulled from active," Zac said, happy to tap away at his laptop. When he glanced at her, he realized she waited for more. His hands flew up. "No idea why. I'm clueless."

"Well, if anyone can suss it out..."

"Better that than, well... I'm not a CSI, Morgan."

Zac's trepidation over the crime scene, the refuse left in the wake of Kane's demise, made her glad to have the room. Local PD had fought her on the case, heated words elevating to the point of fisticuffs until Morgan connected with the FBI for approval.

All the argument had cost her was access to the body, though the autopsy was already scheduled for the following day at the medical examiner's office. She understood the need for a quick turnaround given the prominence of the victim. Plus, she didn't want anyone else's blood on the floor from a fight she could win with her eyes closed.

"Don't worry, Zac," Morgan started. She crouched beside the stained carpet. "I've got this covered."

"I figured since Riley found the lead on this Kane guy he should be involved as well."

"Is that all?" She hadn't spoken to the latest member of the field team in over a week. There had been no need for any interaction. Ever since Bellbrook the team had been in disarray. Lincoln had recovered slowly, but remained silent on the subject of Ruth Heller's death. Morgan had tried to be around for him, yet failed on every level. Ben, though, was another matter. He'd tried approaching her multiple times while hunting down leads in the follow-up to their previous assignment. Each time she had rebuffed him, pushed away just at the sight of him. She didn't see *him* at all, only Bellbrook and what happened.

Only his failure.

She couldn't let that happen again. Not after being put in charge of the case. There was a murder and she was going to solve it. No complications necessary.

"Do you have a problem with Riley being here?" Zac's presence alone took away the simplicity of the case before them. Rather than take the bait, she held her tongue. "Morgan?"

"Leave it, Zac."

He closed the laptop and tucked it away. "Hey. You've been working non-stop for weeks. Ever since Ohio. Taking cases solo whenever you could, leaving everyone else behind as often as possible. Local authorities are more than capable of handling this."

"Like they did in Bellbrook?" Morgan snapped. Brown eyes shot like lasers through the startled analyst. "Kane knew something about what happened to those poor people. Waiting for Riley wasn't an option. Not that it matters now."

Her visit was meant to be a simple interrogation. One stemming from the discovery of the trucking company spotted outside Spring Hill, Kansas: the second site of a spontaneously grown forest derived from the former inhabitants of the town. The trucks and the drivers had vanished, and there was no sign or trace of the individuals responsible for clearing the vast growth of oak trees under the guidance of the Department of Defense.

The trucking company had turned out to be a dead end as well, closed as if it had never existed in the first place. Only it did, and some digging had brought the principal players to light—including Kane, a major shareholder in the firm. The trail had led them here to Shur-Rite, where he stood as their Chief Operating Officer. Their search ended just as it had begun: with frustration and the dead.

"Coincidence?"

Morgan scoffed, hand to her brow.

"Right," the tech muttered. "Big fat no on that one."

They'd learned of Kane's presence back in the country after a jaunt overseas the previous month. Less than a day later the man was dead. How could anyone joke about it being a coincidence?

Someone was covering their tracks, and the DSA was a dozen steps behind them. It grated her worse than Zac's presence or the call for assistance to a man who had yet to earn his stripes in her eyes. Morgan needed to figure it out. She needed the work and *only* the work.

"We should have called ahead," Zac said. "It would have saved you the troubling of leaving HQ."

"Don't call it HQ."

"What do I call it, then?" he asked. "Anyway, I'm just saying you've been a little distant lately and you might want to talk to someone about it."

"Like you?"

He rubbed at his neck awkwardly. "Me? No. I mean, you could if you want to, but—"

"Is that why you're here? Metcalf send you as my personal therapist? Want to know my deep, dark secrets, Zac?"

"What?" His cheeks flushed, and she smirked at his squirming. "No. I told you…"

"What was it again? A vacation to visit your cousin?"

"Second cousin," Zac clarified. "On my mother's side."

"At the *exact* moment I turned up for a case."

"Metcalf called me in," he said with a shrug. "You know how she can be."

"Right."

He cleared his throat. "I'm here to help."

Morgan showed off the crime scene surrounding her. "Feel free."

"From… from a distance," he stuttered. "Like, moral support."

"Just what I need." Or the exact opposite. They were playing games with each other instead of solving a murder. Morgan huffed, pushing through the confused and disoriented Zac into the hallway beyond.

"Hey, where are you going?"

"I'm leaving," she replied with a wave. "You staying?"

"But Riley—"

"Can meet us at the hotel." The elevator dinged and the double doors clanged open. "Same with our contact at the FBI who couldn't bother showing up."

"It's only been—"

"Car's leaving, Modine."

"Coming."

Their descent went quickly and in total silence. Zac fumbled with his equipment. His bag slipped from his shoulder to the ground and spilled notes at her feet. He shuffled them into a pile, still cleaning up when they reached the lobby.

Morgan stepped over him for the front desk and the waiting security guard. "I need a list of visitors from last night."

The middle-aged glorified desk clerk read her ID again, but paused at the agency listed. He shrugged rather than push for more information, clearly overwhelmed by the additional police presence throughout the wing and out front.

"I made some copies."

She took one without a word. A single name was circled.

"Isaac Newton?"

"Kid's idea of a joke. It happens way too often."

"You saw him?"

He removed his hat and scratched at what little remained atop his pale scalp. "Squirrelly kid, yeah. Cops took a sketch."

Morgan peered to Zac and he nodded. "I'll ask."

As he departed she returned to the guard. "Any security feeds?"

"Nothing for the top level," he said. "The lobby has its share though."

She nodded, taking pen to paper. After tearing the sheet off the roll, Morgan handed the note to the man. "We'll be staying at this hotel. Pass this along to anyone looking for us, as well as a copy of the footage."

"Expecting someone?"

She sighed. "More professionals that don't know how to read a clock."

"Got it."

"Thanks."

Zac waited at the front doors, the sketch in hand. She offered a fake clap, which won her a smile from the heavy-handed tech. Why was he there? Why call Riley in on this? She closed her eyes. The growing trees and the cries of the dead were locked in her memory whenever she heard his name. She took a sharp breath of the winter air.

It had been murder, plain and simple. Keeping the case that

way, locking it down to the basics, was all that was required.

And all she wanted from this case.

"What now?" Zac asked.

She held the door open. The breeze cooled her frustration for a brief moment. "Now I want to know everything about this guy. Reginald Kane had skeletons in his closet and one of them got him killed."

CHAPTER FOUR

We have a situation.

It was an understatement to be sure. If he had been called the previous night the appellation might have been appropriate. It would have at least been manageable, especially with his talents and a fair number of payoffs to the local constabulary. His phone, however, had failed to ring until the morning hours. His flight in had stolen even more precious time. Now the only fair assessment ranged from disastrous to a full-blown calamity.

Reginald Kane was dead.

Now he was the doing the calling, the ring incessant against his ear. He tucked close to the shadow around the corner from Shur-Rite for privacy. The line clicked over and a voice answered.

"It's me," the figure at the corner announced.

"How bad is it?"

Two departing agents answered the question. He did not recognize them, and they carried no visible badge or logo. The tall ebony-skinned woman led her flabby colleague away from the crime scene. They passed quickly through the growing police cordon around the block. Flashing lights filled the area, Kane's death muttered in whispers like a growing chorus of condemnation for the job ahead.

The figure cleared his throat, his deep voice booming even as he whispered, "Much worse than I was led to believe. Kane is dead?"

"His removal was necessary for our plans."

"*Our* plans or your own?" The truth of the conversation. They both served agendas behind other agendas. Wheels within wheels, all working against the organization both men served. The figure held ambitions, visions of glory to call his own. So did the man on the other end of the line. For the moment, their paths aligned.

"I need this contained," the voice on the phone said. "Can you do it?"

Questioning his ability was a play of ego, one sorely tempted by the figure hiding in the shadows. The man on the phone wanted a reaction, demanded one with this course. It was a petty tactic. Time was already against them.

"Where is the asset behind this little media frenzy?"

"In the wind," the man said. "She's been reliable in the past. I'm not sure what happened this time."

"They all fail eventually."

"Except you?" A wry smirk carried through the speaker.

"You better hope I don't or your little takeover is dead before it's even begun. If the Trust finds out what you've been doing behind their back you're a dead man."

"See to it they don't."

"I need my team."

The man sighed. "Great. More bodies."

"Only as many as necessary," the figure answered. His mandate was clear. Clean up the mess no matter the cost. When it came to the body count, however, the bureaucrats wanted to hear none of it. They preferred to keep their hands clean and their thoughts untainted by the reality of the work. That went out the window the moment he arrived. Only one aspect remained unclear. "Promethean?"

"Promethean was always a failed notion," the voice said. "Another stray thought from the well. We've managed to tie off most of the loose ends over the years. Go shut down the rest."

"With pleasure." The phone clicked and the figure left the security of the shadows for the street.

The question became how much cleanup was required. Local authority was limited and easily dissuaded from further inquiry. When federal agents turned up, however, the situation skewed to the complicated. And then there were the two strange agents departing the scene to consider.

How much did they know? Were they aware of Kane's connections to Spring Hill and the larger plan?

The shadowy figure needed to know before passing judgment. For that he required access.

A car settled at the corner, away from the police cordon and the bustling crowds. A man in a blue jacket, much too thin for the weather, exited the vehicle and dropped his reports. He scurried to retrieve them, while struggling to keep his badge clipped to his lapel.

The figure at the corner smiled. He had found his access. He journeyed over to assist the agent. "Can I help you with that?"

"I think I've got it," the man said. The papers continued to spread around his ankles, his hands working frantically to keep them contained from the swirling wind. He crouched low, his car obscuring him from view to those up the block. "Really. I can handle it."

"Please." The shadow's deep voice cut through the agent's clumsiness, giving him pause.

"Thanks."

"It's no problem at all," the figure replied. The agent turned to see the dark chasm of the gun's barrel. The silencer minimized the sound of two bullets thudding into the terrified man's chest. He crumpled to the pavement. The figure loomed over his victim with a smile. Quietly, he opened the rear door and lifted the body into the vehicle and out of sight. "I believe you can help with a problem of my own."

CHAPTER FIVE

The recoil stung Lincoln MacKenzie's right arm. His bicep pulsed with pain, even though the wound had long since healed. Every shot caused the same reaction, yet he continued through dozens of exercises along the shooting range in the basement of the DSA warehouse.

Routine had filled his daily life since escaping the clutches of the hospital in the aftermath of the Bellbrook affair. The field team used to call it downtime. A meaningful designation allowing them to turn away from violence, away from the stress that tightened every muscle in their bodies, and away from the destructive nature the DSA labeled as their job.

Instead, Lincoln welcomed the violence. He filled six hours every day with training in the fitness center and unloading a monthly salary's worth of bullets on the specified targets at the end of the shooting range. It did nothing to calm him: the act of ending the life of a paper target. It did nothing to stem the emptiness in his heart over his loss.

Ruth died in Bellbrook, taken by the signal he still failed to understand. She passed alone, when he should have been by her side, no matter what happened to him in the end. Ruth meant that much to him. She must have to deserve such sacrifice on his part, though her memory faded behind the bevy of bullets from the Sig Sauer tight in his grip.

There had been joy, pure joy with her. Their time together, albeit short, filled his days with warmth. A comfort unfelt since childhood, since the death of his mother.

Now another loss took the feeling from him.

The joy faded, and the memory of such an emotion slipped

with each day spent locked in the warehouse of the government organization that had taken him in at his lowest; the place had offered him a life when he imagined all options had vanished due to his mistakes.

Ruth had been a bonus, and a foolish one at that. She had not been part of his personal mission, not part of his plan. She was light, a pure breath of fresh air, unpolluted—at least when they were together. Everything melted away and he imagined nothing better could be possible.

The Sig Sauer emptied, and the trigger clicked loudly against his pulsing finger. The clip unlocked, then slid loose. It clanged against its brethren at his feet. A long breath whistled from his lips and he closed his eyes. The pain filled him and he accepted it, tightening the bicep to force more anguish through his body. He needed the sensation; the pain sustained him on these days of strict routine.

No missions. No grand plan.

All Lincoln held was his anger, and it fueled him.

The retracted target arrived and Lincoln peeled the print from the stand. The chest was no longer visible, and the heart had been eliminated completely from his assault. The head contained a clear pattern, four distinct shots to the brow of the figure.

Bullet-ridden forms collected among the emptied clips and casings. Lincoln extended his arm and rubbed at his wound. The single shot that had forced him to stay behind when he should have been next to Ruth to the very end—together.

The clicking of heels against tile echoed from the hall. The subtle scent of perfume clouded the fading image of Ruth from memory. Lincoln sighed. Heavy hands fell along the tabletop covered with his weapons of choice for the day. Each was from his personal collection—he never borrowed from the extensive armory tucked in the basement of the DSA warehouse.

The clicking halted, but he refused to look, not needing the glare offered by the woman he had avoided for weeks since his return to work. "Say what you came to say and get out."

"Nice. You are aware of how the employer-employee relationship is supposed to function, aren't you?"

Lincoln shuffled the three pistols into his waiting duffel then vacated the range for the staging area near the door. Susan

Metcalf waited by the entrance, leaning along the frame, arms crossed against a chic blazer that accentuated her blue eyes. He dropped the bag on the folding table.

"I think you play the director card enough as it is."

"You know what? I've given you time. I've given you space. What do you want me to say, Lincoln?"

"Ruth is dead!" Lincoln snapped, his anger slipping loose easier than the pull of a trigger. "Grissom too. Who's next for you? Morgan? The new guy?"

She pushed off the frame and started for the hall. "I'm not going to do this with you."

"Seriously," Lincoln pressed, and she stopped. "Answer me. You look at your reports and send us out there to do God knows what day in and day out so, what? We can end up a name on your damn wall?"

"That's enough."

He shook his head. "I wonder if it ever will be for you. We weren't supposed to be there, to be in Bellbrook at all. It was unsanctioned, yet we went. All to satisfy your ego. We *never* should have been there."

"I said, that's enough!" A file slammed on the table between them and her hand spread against the cover. "You want to go this route? Fine. I came to see how your arm was, not play at being your damn counselor. Agents die. Been that way since before my time. Will be that way long after. You can be pissed at me as much as you want, but you know damn well you're not really mad at me, so suck it up and do your job."

"How?" Lincoln raged. "I'm off the active roster. Hell, even Modine is playing field agent for you. And I'm stuck here. So tell me again how you're not my damn counselor and let me *do* something!"

Her tongue ran the length of her bottom teeth, holding a breath. "I want to hear it first."

"Hear what?"

"Ruth Heller," she said. "I want to hear it from you."

Lincoln dropped the duffel's straps. The bag slammed to his feet. "You knew?"

"You thought I didn't? That I suddenly lost the ability to see what was right in front of my face? What you two were doing?"

"That was none of your—"

"Of course it was!" Metcalf bellowed, finger at his chest. "What the hell were you thinking? You compromised this team with your little tryst, Lincoln, and I—"

"Shut it," Lincoln said, batting her hand away. "Shut your mouth."

"No, Agent MacKenzie," she continued. "I won't. You were recruited to do a job. You had nothing when Grissom approached you. We gave you a purpose again, and you blew it. Own up to it. Tell me what I want to hear."

She wasn't wrong. Much as he wanted to snap her neck—and he imagined the act repeatedly as she spoke—her words were never false. He needed the job, the work the DSA provided. It was a chance to redeem himself, one he could never truly earn given a lifetime of service.

Ruth had never diminished those needs; she'd simply offered another path in the darkness of his life. It had been a chance to live a life never afforded him previously. Was it a delusion, a mirage, in the great desert of their existence? He never had the chance to find out. She had been taken before he understood the truth.

She left him with only the job and his hate.

"I was sleeping with Ruth."

Metcalf's eyes softened. Her hand reached for his shoulder. "I know. I'm sorry for your loss."

He nodded, but turned away. "We done here?"

"Not even close."

"Metcalf—"

"Director," she corrected.

"Cute," Lincoln replied. "I fall back in line and get to play with others again?"

"No."

"No?"

She patted the file on the table. "I have something else for you."

"Reassignment?" Lincoln exclaimed in disgust. "Dammit, Met—"

"Director," she cut him off. The file opened and she slid it his way. "And it isn't reassignment. More like an extension of your last. There were loose ends from Bellbrook. The rest of the field team is handling one of them, and I need you to take care of this part. No one else can find out. Understand?"

Another unsanctioned operation. Another secret. Metcalf was full of them, and she now expected him to carry on the same, as if the last one hadn't cost them all dearly. As if any came without a price.

That was never why he came aboard. He had joined the DSA to continue to serve his country with honor, the way he had in the Army. For him, it was never about a single agenda, but something grander—an ideal.

"What the hell is this now?" The opened file rested before him, classified documents to the left. On the right-hand page, clipped to the top, was a single image of a man. Rounded spectacles hid his eyes and a sneer-like smile on his face. "This is him?"

"The man from Bellbrook," Metcalf said. "The so-called Witness."

"Where did this image come from?"

"There are more. From various points in Ohio in the days leading up to the event. He was careful, but look hard enough and—"

"That's what I'm doing now?" he asked. Thick fingers tightened along the corners of the image of the man who had taken Ruth from the world. "Looking for a shadow?"

"*Finding* a shadow," Metcalf clarified. "A player like this? As smart as he is?"

"He's been around a while."

Metcalf nodded. "Stephanie is running facial recognition."

"Your secretary?" Lincoln asked. "We have over two hundred analysts that want to bury this guy next to the Hitlers and Bin Ladens of the world and you've put the least qualified person on the job?"

"You'd be surprised to learn her qualifications," Metcalf objected. "And I believe I stated the confidential nature of this mission. You are not the only person looking for this man."

Lincoln hesitated. A target, and a ticking clock. Wasn't this what he wanted? What he'd been asking for every day since Ruth's death?

Metcalf shifted next to him, grazing the image lightly. "Stephanie is to be your one and only point of contact on this."

He nodded. She handed the file over and he tucked it in the

waiting duffel. "When I find him?"

Metcalf stopped at the door. "There's a reason you're the one looking."

"I'm going to need to hear the words, Director."

"End him, Agent MacKenzie," Metcalf said in a clear tone. "He did more than wipe Bellbrook off the map: he killed one of our own. You find him, and you end him."

CHAPTER SIX

You find him, and you end him.

She said those words: words she never thought she would utter, words of hate and anger. They were words which displayed a lack of control—another impossibility.

Metcalf made her way to the waiting area outside of her office before her legs turned to jelly—she believed the floor would greet her if she attempted another step. Her body quaked, fraught with emotion at the directive given to Lincoln—and at the excitement dancing in his eyes at the possibility ahead.

End him.

Kill the Witness.

Metcalf used her personal assistant's vacant counter to stabilize herself. Deep, cleansing breaths flowed through her. Yet the edict remained, as set in stone as the image in her grasp. She stared into the empty orbs hidden behind opaque lenses and tried to understand the actions of the figure caught in the frame.

Seven thousand people had lost their lives thanks to his deeds, thanks to the signal he unleashed on the unsuspecting populace. How could she not have seen it coming? How had she been so blindsided, so unprepared, when it had finally happened?

Fingers crushed the image of the man in the black suit and fedora. His image distorted and twisted from view, yet her grip tightened—demanding answers and explanations, yet only hearing silence in the wind.

When the door opened to her office, Metcalf dropped the photo. The crumpled wad skittered along the counter before rolling across the floor at the newcomer to the waiting area.

"Oh. Director, I didn't..." Stephanie Atwater crouched to retrieve the item and tossed it in the waiting receptacle. She flattened her skirt then rounded the counter. "Is everything all right?"

"It will be." Metcalf's gaze fixed on the tossed image, handled neatly and quickly. If only real life occurred in the same fashion. "You're on your way?"

"Yes," her assistant replied. "The search is still running. Is Lincoln—?"

"Ready and waiting."

Stephanie's hand fell on the file between them. "Are you sure this is the right...?" Silence ended her question. It wasn't her place, and she recognized the line immediately. Sharp blue eyes met her, the cold, unforgiving stare which greeted most these days. Stephanie offered an apologetic nod. "Sorry."

Metcalf smirked. Her hand raised Stephanie's chin. "Nothing to apologize for."

"Actually, there is," Stephanie said. She peered back to the open office door. "You have company."

The director shuffled around the corner, catching sight of her waiting guest, and sighed. "I see."

"Do you want me to handle it?"

"No." Hesitation gripped her for an instant. *If only it were that easy...* "Besides, you have other priorities."

Stephanie gathered her belongings and slung her purse over her shoulder. "I'll be in briefing if you need anything."

"Thank you."

He stood at the far side of her office, and wore a white sport coat and khakis. His hands were clasped along his back. Before him was a framed painting of a yellow farmhouse with white trim adorning a wraparound porch.

"I can see why you would enjoy this in here," he said without looking. "A calming retreat. Who was the artist?"

"No one you would know." Metcalf stopped at her desk. She tucked the file on the Witness into her drawer. She shut it tight as her guest turned to greet her.

"Director Metcalf," David Hollis beamed. He offered his hand and approached exuberantly. "A pleasure. Sorry to drop in unannounced."

Hollis. The name stung. For as much as their paths connected through multiple agencies, they had managed to avoid each other for much of their careers. She preferred it that way.

Ignoring his hand, Metcalf circled the room. "What can I do for you, Mr. Hollis?"

His hand fell, but his enthusiasm remained. "Quite the operation you have running here. Top-notch talent. Your closed-case ratio is leagues above other agencies I've visited in the past year. You should be proud."

"I am," she answered, quicker than intended. Metcalf steadied her nerves. Her hand squeezed the cushion on the back of her desk chair. "Now if you've finished the empty compliment portion of this discussion?"

"Susan, I—"

"You had it right the first time," she said. "Director Metcalf."

"Of course," Hollis said, a short shrug of recognition at her irritation. "I merely wished to stop by to offer my services should you ever—"

She stopped him with the shake of her head. "I know all about your services, Mr. Hollis."

"I sincerely doubt that."

Fists clenched, the demure director shifted for a glass of water. A silent offer extended through the raising of the pitcher, one declined by the uninvited intruder in her midst. Hollis was a snake, a serpent in the grass, playing for an audience and more: access to her department. It was the same way he entered every other agency in the system, secret or otherwise. He brought knowledge, the most powerful of weapons in their business.

She wanted nothing to do with him. After pouring her glass to the brim, Metcalf lifted the clear liquid and savored a long sip before rejoining him at the lone desk in the center of the office.

"You're an outside consultant pushing an outside agenda, Mr. Hollis," she started, monotone—as if she were reading his biography in the back of a book. "You keep your own counsel and set your own path. Every time those cross my doorstep there seems to be trouble on the horizon. So why don't you skip the dance and spell it out for me?"

"An interesting perspective. One not shared by your former colleague, Agent Grissom."

"What did you say?"

"He sought my counsel from time to time. I have incredible

resources at my disposal and availed myself when necessary."

"I doubt that," Metcalf asserted. There was no way Grissom would have done anything of the sort. Everything they did at the DSA was above board. Every choice was shared with the other. No secrets were kept.

"You're more than welcome to believe what you will," Hollis continued. He reached for his briefcase. He clicked open the latch, then removed a single item from within. "Here."

A file extended from his well-manicured fingers and she took it in hand. "A present for me? And here I didn't get you any-thing."

"It's my final report."

A month earlier it had been called an inquiry, one looking in-to Grissom's death. Hollis had been brought in by the Inter-Agency Council to find a scapegoat—a pointless exercise. Metcalf knew who was at fault for the operation.

After sitting for a closer look, she slipped her reading glasses in place. Her fingers danced along the cover and the shiny label at the center. "The Grissom File. Catchy title."

Hollis' grin faded. Hands leaned along the edge of the desk and aggravation set in. "A man *died*, Director. Grissom fell dur-ing a routine operation and you—"

"Don't," Metcalf snapped. "Don't justify your actions to me. You've divided this department enough with your interviews and your prodding. Take it up with your masters at the Council if you have anything further to say."

Hollis left the desk, straightening his sport coat. He reclaimed his briefcase, then snapped the clasp shut. "I thought you might like a copy first. Apologies for the inconvenience."

He started for the door and she let out a long sigh. She rubbed her eyes behind her glasses and called after him. "What is it?"

"Excuse me?"

"Your final assessment." She hated to ask, hated the thought of the question. Her doubts remained regarding the order given to leave the infected Grissom behind for the greater good, even though her team had thought differently. She had made the call and the decision had left her barren.

"I leave it up to the Council," Hollis said. "They have final say on these matters."

A non-answer, the true one tucked behind sharpened incisors on full display. "Of course."

"By the way, how goes the search?" he asked, approaching once more. "For Agent Heller's replacement? I was saddened to hear of her loss."

"I'm working on it."

He nodded in understanding. "The Council is eager to weigh in. Even offered some options, from what I've heard. Proper protocol and all that. Unlike your recent recruitment of... what was his name again?"

"Riley."

"Yes. Benjamin Riley." The name boomed in the room. Hollis' hand grazed his chin curiously. "Scandalous business in Buffalo. Convicted of several crimes if I understand the situation correctly?"

"He was set up."

"Was he, now? He must have been playing a dangerous game indeed to deserve such effort, don't you think?"

"I wouldn't know," she said. The man's thin glare cut through her. "We're still looking into what really happened."

"I'm sure you are," Hollis responded. "Ah, well, he's not who *I* would have selected for the position."

"Wasn't your call."

"Or yours," he reminded her. "Not without approval."

"Now you listen to me." Metcalf stood, ripping the glasses from her face. Her cheeks flushed. Her fist clenched. Defense of Agent Riley brimmed to the surface, but she held it back at the sight of the man's swagger. He wanted the reaction, demanded the argument.

She refused to humor him, and instead cleared her throat. "I'll be sure to defer to the Council's protocol next time."

"Wonderful." His smile widened at her acceptance. He reveled in her verbal surrender. He started for the door. "I hope we can do this again soon."

"And I hope to never see your smug face again, Mr. Hollis," Metcalf said.

He nodded. The lights from the hall outside cast him in shadow, thick blackness covering her office. "Yes, well, I'm not so sure that will be possible, Susan. After all, the future always manages to surprise us in the most unusual ways."

CHAPTER SEVEN

Ben hesitated at the motel door, where the faded 7 slanted to the right as it hung limply from the nail in the center. His bag sat at his side, his sidearm tight to his hip. The work called, yet still he stood by, waiting for a clear sign of what was the right choice.

The DSA needed him and right now he needed the work, needed their resources to find out who had framed him and taken his life away. But how long would that arrangement last? They spied on him, watching his every move and questioning his every action. How could he build a life with them? Hell, how could he build even a strand of trust between them with that sticking in the back of his mind?

Tired of the internal debate that followed him from Bethesda to the streets of Chicago, Ben tapped on the door. It swung open and Zac Modine's scowl greeted him.

"Somebody order an extra-large with everything?" Ben asked.

The tech sighed. "What took you so long?"

The newcomer closed the door behind him. He tucked his bag under the small desk in the corner. "Oh to be loved and treasured."

"You'll get used to it," Morgan replied without looking. Her eyes cast deep shadows, glowering at the photos spread across the full-size mattress on the far side of the room. Every image contained the same crime scene: what appeared to be a murder.

"You keep saying that," Ben said with a wasted grin. Zac clacked needlessly on his keyboard, and Morgan's preoccupation bordered on rude.

"It might happen."

"Doubtful," Zac interjected. "So what kept you?"

Ben shook his head. "Have you seen the traffic in this city? Also, and this is more to the point... I had no idea where I was going. Stopped at the Shur-Rite Building. You weren't there. Went to the hotel using the info you left with the guard. Again, you weren't there."

"Rats."

"Okay, Charlie Brown."

"No," Zac clarified. "It had so many rats. As long as Morgan's forearm."

"I made him find other accommodations."

"Good call." Ben settled at the edge of the bed closest to the door, splitting the room between the two colleagues. He dug into his pocket and removed a flash drive. It sailed toward the table and Zac's waiting hand. "Security footage you requested."

"Perfect." He popped the drive into the side of his laptop to start the download.

"When did you two—?"

"This morning," Zac interrupted. The tech took a long swig of a mammoth bottle of soda, his gaze drawn to the lanky woman clearly uninterested in their presence. Concern sat in his mud-brown eyes.

"Okay," Ben said, drawing out the word. "So what am I doing here, then? A second pair of—?"

"Yes."

Ben turned to Morgan. "Can he stop doing that?"

"Probably not."

"Then can I ask why *he's* here? In the field, I mean? Being all agenty?"

"Vacation."

"Really?"

"I was."

"Where's Claire?" Ben's arms crossed his chest.

"Who?"

"Your wife?"

Zac leaned back. "How do you know about my wife?"

"How do you *not* know about your wife?" Ben shot back, matching the nasal tone of his colleague.

"He was here," Morgan said. "We're following up on Reginald Kane."

"The trucking-company guy?" Surprise jumped in his voice. He'd found Kane during a routine search of a group of missing truckers from three weeks back. They had been bought and paid for by a company out of South Bend. Kane had sat on their board of directors. "He was out of the country."

"Not anymore."

"You found him? You spoke with him?"

Morgan shook her head. "He's dead."

She passed over a photo from the bed and he took it without a glance. "Dead?"

"It turns out the trucking operation wasn't his only business. He also played shareholder to a number of other companies, in addition to serving as the Chief Operating Officer of Shur-Rite Pharmaceuticals." Zac's almost robotic drone caused the drowsiness in Ben to return, but he fought through it, the dead man's image still caught in his grasp.

"Someone was waiting for him?"

"Last night."

The photo dropped to his side. "And the trucks? Were you able to find the connection back to Spring Hill? Or locate the missing truckers?"

"The trucking firm has been shuttered," Morgan said. "That was my first stop."

"Another dead end," Ben said with a grimace. It had been a month's worth of them since Bellbrook. Since a man known as the Witness had taken the lives of seven thousand people for a simple test. The test had connected to another site in Spring Hill, where the Department of Defense was stationed and completely aware of the situation. Ben took a sharp breath. "So why are we still here?"

Anger crept in Morgan's voice. "A man is dead."

"A scumbag possibly involved in the deaths of thousands," Ben retorted.

"He was killed."

"And homicide is under our mandate now? We should be looking elsewhere for what happened in Bellbrook. We still haven't closed that case."

"We are," Morgan snapped. She stood. After picking up the dropped photo, she placed it in his hand once more. "Look closer, Riley."

A charred corpse stared back. It was a heap of bones and ash. Flesh from the body ran like thick mucus to the carpet. Kane's absent eyes pleaded for mercy never to be given.

"He burned to death."

Zac shook his head. "Yet there was no damage to the room except for the spot where he fell?"

The newcomer hesitated. Slowly, Ben picked his way through the images littering the neighboring bed. The office appeared pristine beyond the circle of destruction near the entrance. It looked completely untouched, as if the photos had been taken at a different time.

"Your point?" Ben pressed. "Fires happen, Zac."

"That controlled?" Irritation crept in Morgan's every word. "And Kane just sat there and fried?"

Zac joined her. "No accelerant. No source of ignition."

"Okay," Ben said, hands in surrender. "How about spontaneous—"

"Don't say it," Zac answered before Morgan had her chance to swat the idea down.

"His arm, Riley." The photo was back in her hand, pointing to the object in question. "Look at his arm."

Amid the tissue residue and the discoloration of Kane, the ulna of the man's right arm held deep grooves along the bone. Grooves in a uniform pattern.

"A hand?"

"Welcome to the crime scene, Riley."

He didn't understand her anger. The weariness in her face surprised him as well. They had worked in different circles since the Bellbrook incident, but he thought they did well together— especially considering the circumstances of their inaugural case.

Unfortunately, it seemed his opinion was in the minority. That needed to change, though he faltered at finding a way through her demeanor. His every joke stoked a fire greater than the one that took Reginald Kane from the world.

"I appreciate you having me, Morgan. But are we really talking about a Johnny Storm wannabe here?"

"I will add Jim Hammond to the suspect list as well," Zac noted to a pair of blank stares. "What? No props."

"No one says props anymore."

"They don't?"

"No," Morgan confirmed. "And Agent Riley here is just up-set he got out-nerded."

"Am not," Ben whined. He sighed, then raised his hand. "Fi-ne. Props."

Morgan's clenched fists fell to her hips and she returned to the normalcy of the crime scene photos. "Honestly, I'm not sure why either of you talk. No one knows what the hell you're on about half the time anyway."

"This is true," Zac said. "I've reached out to HQ to see if there have been any similar situations noted in the Archive."

"Don't call it HQ," Ben said with a smirk.

"The Hub?"

"Zac..." Morgan groaned.

He ignored her. "Station One?"

"Zac!"

"Right." He leaned close to Ben. "We can spitball later."

"Let's not," Morgan said. "Dinner?"

Zac took the hint. Grabbing his phone, he started for the door to call in an order. "Right."

Ben waited for the door to close before falling against the bed. "How long have they kept Zac in that warehouse they call an office?"

"He's fine." A long breath escaped her. "He'll be fine."

Ben wasn't so sure. Zac's presence concerned him—not for the case at hand, but for the trouble back at home. The bugs in his apartment were sophisticated tech, the kind thrown around like toys by the analyst in their midst. The far-fetched coinci-dence of his so-called vacation did little to assuage Ben's grow-ing paranoia.

Morgan didn't help matters either. She rubbed her neck, put-ting her back to him. "I need a shower after today."

Staring at death held that effect on him as well. He shot out of the bed and stood beside her. "I should have been included in this from the start, Morgan. This was *my* lead."

"I'm aware." Her gaze caught his, locking him in her brown eyes. He had seen pain in them, terror in the heart of Bellbrook and sadness at their shared loss. None of that remained. Not since he'd stumbled out of the forest alone—without Ruth. Since then only one emotion had filled them—when she wasn't avoid-ing him. "You're here now. So help solve this or get out of my way."

"Wow." Ben took a step back. "Guess I should have brought that pizza after all."

Morgan moved away from him. In front of the vanity mirror she pulled her curled strands of black to the back and tied them off. "I'm meeting with the medical examiner tomorrow for a closer look at Kane. I'll see if we can get any prints off the mark left on his arm."

"Morgan, listen—"

"Guys," Zac called. The door creaked open, and his shadow was cast across the room.

"Let it drop," Morgan said. "It's been a long day."

"I don't think that's all there is to it."

"Guys!" Zac yelled once more.

"What is it?"

Both turned to the door. Zac's hands rose above his head, fingers outstretched. "Little help here?"

Behind him a man entered the room, gun pressed against the back of the tech's head. His thin jacket of dark blue hugged muscular arms and shoulders. Three bright yellow letters adorning the jacket beamed under the lights of the room.

F.B.I.

"Hands where I can see them!" the man shouted. "Do it now!"

CHAPTER EIGHT

"ID! Now!" The federal agent with the gun to the back of Zac's head stepped into the motel room and everything went straight to hell.

Morgan blamed herself. As lead agent in the field, the burden fell to her. Ruth had struggled with the same issues—utilizing her team to the best of their abilities. Morgan needed Ben and Zac to play to their strengths for the betterment of the case. Unfortunately, she knew of no strength in either one, their weaknesses far too numerous.

"Guys?" Zac's hands waved in the air. Panic sat in his eyes, his presence in the affair questioned by all. This situation was proof of his inexperience; the tech's proficiency centered on the warehouse headquarters—definitely not *HQ*—of the DSA. "He's pointing a gun at me. Why is he pointing a gun at me?"

"I don't see a problem with that," Ben joked—the only tone the man seemed to convey. Snark and sarcasm were his default weapons. It made Morgan's blood boil and she struggled to restrain her anger.

"Riley…"

Ben's hand edged for his hip, but she shook her head. He tracked her gaze, their friendly neighborhood federal agent following the exchange closely. Ben started for his breast pocket. "I'm reaching for my badge. Let's all take a breath."

"Hurry it up, Riley," Zac pleaded. "I'm allergic to violence. Especially violence aimed at my head."

Ben's jaw clenched. "If I hurry our friend might get nervous. Do you want him nervous?"

Morgan interjected, "Look, there's no reason for this,

Agent...?"

"Hendricks," the man answered. "And I'll determine that for myself, thank you. Care to explain why you showed up at an open crime scene without jurisdiction like you own the place?"

Ben tilted his head, eyebrow raised. "You did call the local branch, right?"

"I did," Morgan said with a grimace. "Our point of contact was late."

"There was traffic," Hendricks said.

"See?" Ben exclaimed. "This city, right?"

"Don't bond with him, Riley," Zac said.

Ben removed his ID and tossed it to the edge of the bed in front of them. "If you have to shoot him, I'll understand."

"Not. Funny," Zac said.

Morgan rolled her eyes. Working with Ben was never going to work, this exchange proof of that on every level. She needed to focus on the operation, and his inability to respect what was happening made that impossible.

She removed her badge and flipped it open. "We're DSA, here investigating a case that led us to Reginald Kane."

Hendricks pushed Zac away and snatched Ben's ID from the bed. He looked it over curiously, then tossed it back to Ben. His gun lowered before returning to the waiting holster strapped to his hip.

"Kane's dead."

Ben winced. "Not the best timing on our part."

"DSA?" Hendricks said with a sigh. "They called the *SAD* agents in on this?"

"Sad agents?" Ben fought back a laugh. "Did anyone actually think before they named this department?"

"Yeah," Zac replied, hands still over his head. "Geriatric bureaucrats smoking cigars in dark rooms figuring out how many kids they can name after themselves. Creativity not required."

"Put your arms down, Zac. You look ridiculous."

Zac lowered his hands. He circled the small table in the corner before settling into the waiting chair. Morgan closed her badge.

"I'm curious how you are aware of us, Agent Hendricks?"

"Connor." A gravelly edge to his voice made the name echo in the silence of the room. "Rumor, mostly. Office talk about consultants helping out on the stranger workload that has been cropping up more and more frequently."

"We're water-cooler talk now?" Zac huffed.

"Great government secret."

"Two words that never belong in the same sentence."

"Great?"

"Guys!" Morgan shouted in frustration. Hendricks laughed, though he fell silent at the glare offered by the woman with the curly ebony locks. Morgan took a deep breath, hand to her chest. "Agents Dunleavy and Riley. And this here is Zac, our technical support."

Hendricks nodded. "Sorry about the snafu earlier."

"Not a problem."

"Quick question," Ben jumped in.

"Riley, now isn't—" Morgan stopped, gnawing lightly on her lower lip.

"Sorry," he continued. "Just curious why the FBI is involved in a homicide case?"

"Kane?" Hendricks said. "That really why you're here?"

"You're not?"

Hendricks shook his head. "The fire that killed him? It's not the first. Eight in the last four years. Usually in a clinic or lab though. No victims."

"And they match?" asked Morgan, curiosity spiking.

"No accelerant. No device. No reason for the fire to start or for Mr. Kane to flame on."

"Not a word," Morgan snapped as Zac and Ben grinned, sharing the joke. Both turned to her in surprise and she rolled her eyes. "What? Please. I have a nephew."

"Well," Zac said as he cracked his knuckles over his keyboard. "The arson angle definitely gives us more to play with."

He dug in, typing furiously on his keyboard. Morgan waited for Ben to comment on the awkward silence permeating the room. Her assumption frustrated her almost as much as the man himself. Why did his presence aggravate her? Why was she so quick to jump down his throat more than anyone she had known since joining up with the agency?

"Wow," Zac muttered, breaking the momentary quiet. They waited for more. When silence returned, Morgan cleared her throat. Zac stopped his reading. "Right. I'm not reading aloud, am I?" He spun the monitor around, cases in multiple windows spread across the screen. "In broad strokes, it looks like four of the sites Agent Hendricks alluded to were medical research facilities. Drug trials and the like for different companies. Two were even off-site labs for pharmaceutical companies like Shur-Rite."

"They seem connected to me," Ben admitted.

Hendricks nodded. "Information about their work has been slim. Servers wiped. People too scared to talk. For what reason, I have no idea. But I'll run them down again. See if something new pops up. Seriously, though, if this is anything like the other scenes there won't be anything and all you'll get is a couple days of Chicago hospitality for your trouble." Hendricks reached for the complementary notepad in the room and jotted down his number, tearing it loose and handing it to Morgan. "If you find anything."

She passed along a business card in return. "We'll keep working our leads, then."

"Anything of note?"

"Not right—"

"We're checking security feeds at the moment," Zac interrupted. "Seeing who comes up from Shur-Rite, then matching them to the names from the log and the sketch taken from the guard's description."

Morgan sighed. Zac read her irritation and clammed up immediately, though the damage had been done. Why it mattered surprised her, as so much had this night. There was something about Hendricks though, from his cold stare to the deep edge to his voice. Something didn't add up.

"Shur-Rite gave you their files already?"

"I asked nicely."

"Perfect."

"We'll be in touch, then," Ben said. He nodded to the open door of the motel room.

"Sounds good." Hendricks took the handle and closed the door behind him. Warmth returned to the room, and each of them finally allowed a breath to slip free.

Ben fell against the bed then pointed to Zac. "Did you end up ordering food?"

"There was a gun on me!"

"So... that's a no?"

Morgan rubbed her eyes. "I'm going to bed."

"Sounds like a plan," Ben agreed.

"Nuh-uh, Johnny-come-lately," Morgan said. Her room waited next door as well as some much needed quiet. "You and the tech wiz are on intel duty for the night."

"You're kidding," Ben called, turning to Zac. "She's kidding, right?"

Zac settled to work. "Menus are on the table. It's going to be a long night, so order heavy."

"Great."

The door closed behind her. "Sweet dreams, you two."

CHAPTER NINE

"Tell me where we're at."

The words reverberated through the briefing room. Though it was usually brimming with top-level technicians and the field team, only two currently occupied the space. Stephanie sat on the far side of the cherry conference table, hands folded before her computer. The DSA logo spun in brilliant digital color above them, the yellows and blues the only light in the room.

Lincoln failed to relax in their solitude. He impatiently stood, hands tight to the side of his chair. Hours slipped away in the waiting game known to his colleagues as 'intelligence gathering.' Wool gathering was more like it. To pass the time, Lincoln returned to the gym for more reps along his aching muscles.

It kept his mind occupied. It kept him centered on his breathing and on his recovery, not on the mission handed down by Metcalf. She had ordered the death of the Witness. He accepted it, wholeheartedly. To Lincoln, it was the only acceptable solution for what the man had done.

All they had to do now was find the bastard.

Stephanie was a beautiful woman, flawless skin and perfectly crafted features. Thin, yet packing power underneath her plaid-skirt-and-stockings combination, she carried herself confidently in his presence. Very few were able to pull that off in the department. When she'd called he didn't hesitate to drop everything.

"I've been looking over everything available since the director passed the assignment to me," she started. "Hundreds of hours of satellite feeds all poured through our software, starting with Bellbrook and branching out."

"You find him or not?"

Delicate fingers danced along the keyboard, and the display shifted overhead to dozens of images lifted from the system of a single individual: The Witness on a street corner in New York City, attending a film opening in Los Angeles, and another on a tour of the Washington Monument. He was everywhere.

"Dammit..."

"Now, Lincoln—"

He stopped her with a cold stare. "Don't, kid. I'm not looking for a pep talk here."

"Hey, I know what this guy means to you," Stephanie pressed. "I also understand what you and the director, hell, what everyone is going through because of what this guy did. But I have to disagree on your objective here."

"Then you don't really understand anything do you?"

"Now that isn't—"

"Metcalf put you in the chair, Atwater. Now show me the target already."

It was more anger than he had meant. She didn't deserve it either. For as much as Metcalf trusted Stephanie, she was nothing more than a glorified secretary. Not an operative, and certainly not a killer. She couldn't understand what was at stake, the level of pain Lincoln contained thanks to one man's actions.

No one else would die because of him. Not if Lincoln found him first.

She hesitated before highlighting a series of photos, each taking front and center on the holographic display over the conference table. "This is the most recent footage I was able to locate. It's from the Central Library in Lexington, Kentucky. He made three separate visits, and all within the last week."

In each, the man's back was turned to the camera. All, however, clearly depicted the same individual as the rest. He wore his signature fedora and black suit. That wasn't enough for Lincoln. He waited until he saw the man's face—the circular frames of the man's glasses and his arrogant sneer—before confirming the target.

"Why there?" he asked.

She shrugged, the information unavailable from the images provided. "Internal feeds show him hanging out in the historical archive section with each visit. Never takes anything out of the library. Never interacts with any personnel or visitors."

"He knows where the cameras are."

"All of them," Stephanie confirmed. "You think it might be a trap?"

There was no question about it. "Doesn't matter. It's a start."

He moved for the door, and Stephanie jumped to her feet. "Lincoln, wait. I could —"

"Keep tracking him," he said. "I've got this."

"It won't bring her back."

His hand turned the knob hard, and the light from the hall immediately poured into the room. He peered back, his eyes cold and dark against the sudden illumination.

"It doesn't have to."

"Then what is this all about?"

He closed the door behind him without answering. If she couldn't see the situation for what it was then the problem lay with her and not him. His mission was clear and he would execute it to the fullest of his abilities.

A gift for Ruth. Revenge at her passing, and for those lost a month ago to the great forest of Bellbrook. Closure at last.

His bags waited in his locker and he started for them immediately, not allowing another second to pass. The sound of the door to Operations closing in tandem with his own stopped his progress before it began.

"MacKenzie?" He turned to see Deputy Director Greg Sullivan approaching. The man in his mid-fifties wore a sweater vest and his neatly trimmed beard proudly. Another bureaucrat in a department needing soldiers.

"Sir?"

"I didn't expect to find you here at this hour."

Lincoln nodded. "I could say the same."

The deputy director rubbed his beard. "I was hoping to check in with Zac. Any idea where he might be?"

"In the field."

"I'm sorry? My hearing must be going."

"You should get that looked at."

Sullivan stopped him from passing, curiosity in his eyes. "You're serious?"

"I am."

"And you?" His hand fell away, then pointed to the closed

door down the hall. "An unscheduled briefing? Has something happened I should—"

"After action reports," Lincoln interrupted quickly. "I was reviewing relevant intel from the Bellbrook incident. You know, busy work."

"It's been over a month though," Sullivan said. "Why would you still be off the active roster?"

"Not my decision to make."

Sullivan shook his head. "Let me talk to Susan on your behalf. Get this straightened out."

"I can speak for myself. Thanks though."

"Not a problem," the man replied. "Things haven't been working well since… well, since Agent Grissom, have they? The DSA stands for a noble purpose. I hope to continue that, even if we've gone astray of late."

Bellbrook. The unsanctioned operation had left the DSA vulnerable to Inter-Agency Council oversight. Lincoln didn't require a fancy degree to read the opportunity written on Sullivan's face. He saw blood in the water and was looking for other sharks in the sea.

"Same here," Lincoln answered.

"I could help with the reports," Sullivan said. "Make sure they're up to snuff for the Council?"

"I've got it covered."

Sullivan nodded. He patted the man's shoulder, leaning close. "I'm here to help, Lincoln. In any way I can."

"I'll keep it in mind, sir," the soldier said. Sullivan smiled, the gesture practiced and false. He continued down the hall, leaving Lincoln to the quiet of the basement level of the DSA.

He didn't need help. He didn't need anything except the Witness at the barrel end of his sidearm. One shot, the pain of the recoil, and then?

Mission accomplished.

"I'll keep it in mind."

CHAPTER TEN

Henry straightened the ID card on his shirt. The third button on his blue polo slipped loose and he redid the troublesome item, his reflection in the glass doors leading to the Jen-Pad Incorporated lobby shining in the morning sun.

His hair was slicked back by a wet comb. The shower at the local YMCA had done little to wake him from a fitful night of sleep, though it had succeeded in making him presentable for work.

For the first time since sneaking out of the Shur-Rite Building, Henry caught his breath. He had returned home, quiet to avoid any chance of waking his mother. Not that much could rouse her at this point. The medication saw to that. Still, he snuck through the home, collecting the late-night delivery box and tossing it into the garbage. The contents of the box and the stacks of cash found at the bottom were slipped into the back of his closet along with one other souvenir from his trip downtown.

Reginald Kane's gun rested beside the blood money earned from the deed. Henry had wanted to leave it at the scene, but concern won out. Instead, he tucked the weapon away and buried it where his mother would never find it, before racing back out into the night to figure things out.

Distance, however, failed to bring clarity. A long day of hiding—filled with nightmares—condemned any chance at rest and sent his thoughts spiraling, replaying the events with Kane in an endless loop.

His mother finally called. Text messages followed the ignored calls. Requests for medication soon turned into pleas for a simple reply—an acknowledgment of his location and situation. When he finally worked up the courage to answer, the questions began. He lied, as all good sons would in his place. Henry claimed work as the reason for his absence from their home all day.

It was a new job and required a whole explanation, the details falling short of describing his role with the pharmaceutical company. In her eyes a top-level position was expected, his brilliance having been on full display throughout his time in school. When Henry had declined to continue his education at the collegiate level his opportunities had diminished, not that he sought many out. His condition made that impractical, to say the least. The lower, more menial, tasks of the working world helped keep his secret safe.

The job was necessary—any job really—but the current one fit his needs perfectly. Jen-Pad allowed him to earn enough to cover his mother's medicine while also giving him the social outlet he tried to deny himself for fear of the outcome.

Medicine took priority over all others. For the longest time, his mother had maintained their household doing odd jobs. Nothing regular or steady, she would just help out a friend here or there to keep the mortgage company content. It was never a privileged life, though it was one Henry recognized as vital, one full of sacrifice by the loving woman who had brought him into this world.

He could do no less for her now when she needed him.

Of course, his hope to help came at a price, and a man had died from his actions. The terror in Kane's eyes, the scent of burning flesh, followed Henry through the lobby of Jen-Pad, past the curious security guard on duty, to the janitorial supply room at the end of the corridor.

The door opened as he reached for it. Bob Patterson greeted him with a wide grin. "Henry! Feeling better?"

Bob's excitement for the work was only matched by his girth. As Henry's direct supervisor, he stood as an infectious leader, constantly focused on morale over the job at hand. He had handled Henry's interview and mentored him every step of the way to make sure the young man felt at ease at Jen-Pad.

Mostly, his presence made Henry feel normal, which was something relatively rare. The young man smiled, ushered into the supply room with gusto by the waiting supervisor.

"Yes, sir," Henry said. "It must have been a twenty-four-hour thing."

"Those are the worst," Bob replied, picking at crumbs in his thick goatee. "I remember one time Winnie undercooked the meatloaf. I think I became a permanent resident of the downstairs bathroom. Not what you want to hear, I'm sure."

"Sorry again about calling in yesterday like that."

"I do prefer employees to work a full week before I scare them off." Bob rested his hands on his hips, looming over the new recruit. Then a fresh grin broke out and he slapped at the young man's shoulder. "Kidding, Henry."

"Oh," Henry said. He nursed the blow to his shoulder and nodded. "Okay."

"You can make it up to me."

Bob reached for a mop. He slid it into the nearest bucket behind the door. The cart rolled in front of Henry, who took the handle from the joyful supervisor, the move slow and cautious.

"That gleam in your eye worries me."

Janitorial work sounded dismal, but for the most part Henry enjoyed the job. It was quiet, and few bothered to hassle him. He took his time with the tasks handed down from Bob, who never complained for a second regarding what was on the docket. Each task simply demanded completion before the next took its place. No questions. No drama. Nice and straightforward, unlike the rest of Jen-Pad.

The place was a pharmaceutical hub for the state. Research took up four of the ten floors. Sales and marketing occupied the third. Executive suites enjoyed the upper levels, though Henry had few reasons to visit them except on the rushed tour from Bob on his first day, which had mostly consisted of the best hiding places for a break rather than a detailed map of the company.

"It should," Bob answered, snapping the young man back to the waiting mop. "We've got a long day ahead of us."

"I could use the distraction."

Bob held him up. "You sure you're okay, Henry? Everything all right at home? Your mom?"

He'd never meant to mention her in the interview. Bob had that welcoming ability to get people to open up. It was probably why he spent more time chatting with employees around the building than working.

Henry had told the man about his mother's condition, the

unexplained nature of her illness, and his concern over it. Whenever he thought of her it brought back the memory of Kane. The terror. The burning. He never should have opened that package when it arrived.

"She's good," Henry lied. His gaze fell away from the boisterous boss. "We're good. Just happy to get to work."

Bob laughed and handed him the schedule for the day. "Say that again after ten hours of bathroom duty."

Henry took the orders in hand. He tucked them in his pocket and squeezed the mop. It was definitely going to be a long day.

CHAPTER ELEVEN

Ben yawned. The effort did little to pull Morgan's attention from the road. The stop-and-go traffic annoyed the pair, their progress barely a crawl through downtown Chicago. Still, he hoped for some connection, some way to open the conversation with the woman at his side. Unfortunately, no sympathy for his long night of information gathering was forthcoming from Morgan.

Ground was covered in quick order thanks to Zac. The analyst with a penchant for eating hit his stride during the second slice of deep dish—supposedly the best in the city, though every menu in the motel room made the claim. The names listed on the visitor log came up empty.

The surveillance footage offered more definite leads. Isaac Newton, the name used on the sign-in sheet, was obviously meant to conceal the visitor's identity. It failed, however, to hide the young man's face from the security monitors. Medium height and build, nervous in his step and his wandering gaze, the kid had been the only visitor to the seventh floor of the Shur-Rite Building. And only minutes before the time of death recorded in the preliminary findings.

Henry Reed. That was the name drawn from their search. A lucky find thanks to the license plate of a truck parked across the street from the building, one the kid had been seen entering after his visit to Shur-Rite.

Zac was into his third slice, burping between keystrokes while attempting to learn more about their newfound suspect. Henry, however, was a ghost in the system. No credit cards. No student loans. No social media trappings permeating the generation. Nothing was gained from their tireless searches, and Ben almost punted the ball to their federal friend, Hendricks, for assistance.

Then Zac found Anna Reed. Henry's mother carried the financial history typically seen when rummaging through someone's digital footprint. That included a current mortgage, which gave them their start.

Morgan listened intently as Ben relayed the information when dawn came. Bleary eyed, Ben hoped for more time to rest. His colleague, however, started for the car with her phone in hand. Hendricks answered, the address was passed along and they were on their way. Ben's sense of obligation won out over his desire for sleep.

"Zac could have come for this," Morgan said. The traffic split and she exited the highway for a residential neighborhood in Rosemont. "Or I could have handled it on my own."

"I'm good," Ben lied, stifling another yawn. "He needed some extra sleep though."

"Was that what he was screaming about when you walked out this morning?"

He smirked. He might have left out the small detail of locking Zac in the bathroom of the motel room. Twelve hours spent with the analyst was more than enough, and Ben wanted the one-on-one time with the woman behind the wheel.

"He'll thank me later," Ben said.

"Doubtful."

"He's not my biggest fan, is he?" It was meant to be a playful question. The answer, though, came in the silence resting on his partner's lips and the cold stare forward rather than meeting him head on. Ben ran his tongue over his teeth. "He's not the only one, I take it."

Morgan turned down a residential side street, noting a black sedan parked in front of the address in question. "I see Hendricks."

They settled along the curb behind their companion, the car silenced. Outside, snow turned to sleet with the morning sun. The mix left muck along the gutter and pools of wet slush throughout the yards. A gray haze surrounded the city. It clearly matched her mood.

Hendricks waited at the sidewalk, umbrella in hand. A dark

trench coat hid his suit and tie combo, standard issue for the federal level.

Morgan reached for the door and Ben stopped her. "Want to talk about it?"

"Talk about what?"

"Mostly the not-talking thing we're doing," Ben said with a disarming grin. "Well, I'd say it's pretty much you, but that would be a bad way to start the conversation."

"Nope." Without another sound, Morgan left the vehicle and slammed the door.

"All right, then," he muttered. "Good talk."

Ben jammed his hands in his pockets, shuffling through the damp grass. His sneakers picked up a trail of mud, and he wiped off chunks on the sidewalk before joining his colleagues in front of the gate leading to the Reed home.

"Agents."

"Been waiting long?" Ben asked.

"Just a minute or so." Hendricks' shoes were wet, but there were also small traces of mud along the heels. Tiny beads of the rain-snow mix flowed down his sleeves despite the umbrella protecting him.

"He in there?" asked Morgan. She pointed to the home.

"No car in the driveway," Hendricks said. "Pick-up seems to be missing. I've put out an APB for it. I did, however, see a light on upstairs when I arrived."

"Could be the mother."

"Not sure. I was about to knock when—"

Shots pierced through the silence of the residential neighborhood. Instinct drove all three low, sidearms drawn and ready.

"Where?" Morgan peered around the area.

"Inside," Hendricks answered as he opened the gate to the property.

"Dammit," Ben cursed, following close.

Morgan took the rear, each covering the other as they sprinted up the walkway for the front stoop. The falling rain muted their approach. Ben moved for the right and pulled open the outer door. Hendricks took the left, leaving Morgan dead center.

She took a breath then nodded to Hendricks. He twisted the knob and pushed. Morgan charged through. Ben and his counterpart had her back in the next moment, both crisscrossing the small foyer to cover all angles.

Silent instructions passed between them. Morgan drove forward down the narrow hall to the kitchen at the end. Hendricks went right into a bedroom. Ben's footfalls were slow as he passed the staircase leading to the upper floor.

There was no presence on the landing. Small wafts of steam rose from the bathroom in the aftermath of a recent shower.

"Anything?" Morgan called, her voice little more than a whisper, yet it carried through the house.

"Clear," Hendricks replied, returning to the foyer.

Ben halted at the entrance to the living room. "Morgan!"

"What is it?" she yelled, rushing to join him.

Sitting in a recliner along the far corner of the room was Anna Reed. Vacant eyes stared at them. Her right hand was limp over the side of the armrest. Small drips of blood streamed down her chest and under her thick, blue bathrobe.

"Move!" Morgan pushed through Ben to the woman's side. She reached for a pulse, looking for some sign of life, a shallow breath, anything to build upon.

Floorboards groaned to the rear of the residence. Steps, quick and skidding along the ground, bounded from the dining room into the kitchen.

"The back door!" Hendricks said.

The door slammed open, blasted by the wind, and returned unable to reconnect with the frame properly. Hendricks raced toward the fleeing suspect, though Ben hesitated between situations.

Morgan turned, clearly frustrated at his lack of movement. "Go!"

He was out the door in the next breath, the warped wood slamming back and forth. The midday gloom temporarily blinded Ben, and his hand hovered over his squinting eyes in an attempt to catch sight of their shooter. A blur of black screeched through the wide alley dividing two residential neighborhoods.

Gunfire thundered in the air, causing the world to snap to high definition for the agent.

Ben jumped the four-foot-high chain-link fence. Hendricks fired at the fleeing vehicle in short bursts. A taillight shattered from the onslaught. Tires squealed over the sound of Ben's shouting as he pulled at Hendricks.

The firing ended and smoke rose from his barrel against the cold. Hendricks shucked off Ben's hand to run after the fleeing sedan. The car, however, took a hard left into traffic. The sound of its roaring engine faded over the din of raging commuters.

"Car was waiting," Hendricks said when Ben joined him at the end of the alley. The irked federal agent jammed his pistol into the holster.

"Was it him?" Ben pressed. The sedan failed to match the surveillance photos found outside Shur-Rite. The Reed family owned a blue pick-up truck. So where had that car come from? "Was it Henry Reed?"

"Yes." Hendricks spun around. His eyes trailed the escape route of the car.

"You sure?"

"It was him," the man snapped. "It was Reed, I'm sure of it."

Ben nodded, letting the question drop. He required more and pushed for information that might go a long way to ending their time in the Windy City. "License plate number?"

"What?"

"The plate number," Ben continued. "We can track it."

Hendricks' jaw fell slack, eyes scurrying to the road. "I..."

"Seriously?"

"I was trying—"

"To be a hero. Got it."

"That's not..." Hendricks trailed off, unable to meet Ben's gaze. "I wasn't—"

"Thinking?" Ben shot back. "We've established that."

Ben didn't like it, didn't care for the narrative growing with each passing moment. "Come on," he said, waving Hendricks back to the Reed home. "Let's hope Morgan has better news."

CHAPTER TWELVE

Morgan's fingers lifted from the carotid artery of Anna Reed's pale body. Nothing. She was gone before their entry to the home. Another life had been lost on their so-called 'simple fact-finding' operation.

Morgan stood, then rounded the coffee table in the spartan living room. Few decorations lined the walls. Fewer photos and keepsakes sat along bookcases and end tables. Dust riddled the furniture, and there was a thick coating on the television stand opposite the recliner that served as Anna's final resting place.

Nothing had been stolen. Nothing stood out of place. Robbery was out of the question in terms of motivation. The timing of the shooting made it completely illogical in the first place. Someone knew they were coming—someone who didn't want Anna Reed speaking to the authorities.

Behind the chair, Morgan crouched and noted three holes in the faded satin finish of the wall. Plaster had been chipped from the impact, the shell casings buried for forensics to dig out. The former physician traced the angle to the back of the chair, noting the three impact points through the cushion; all were made by a .45 caliber weapon—seemingly the same as the one used at the Shur-Rite crime scene.

They were steep angles and Morgan circled around the dead woman to stand before her. She used her fingers as a makeshift substitute for the murder weapon, and took aim. Too steep on the first attempt, Morgan sidled to the other side of the coffee table and tried again. Better, yet still too tall, her six-foot-three build not matching the killer's. She bent lower, shaving a few inches off before angling her pretend weapon once more.

A match.

A six-foot-tall individual was required for the angle achieved. For the shot to be taken the killer had had to enter through the kitchen door at the back of the home, then weave around the sectional sofa, over the ottoman-style end or around the long way, before stopping short of the coffee table and firing. Elaborate, and considering the woman's lack of movement and her comfort in the chair, almost unbelievable.

Why would Anna not stand? Why would she not fight for her life? Her appearance, pasty with deep bags under her eyes, was that of a sick woman. Could that have made the difference? Had she been resting on the chair?

No. The bathrobe disproved that theory immediately. Steam from the bathroom at the top of the stairs greeted them upon their arrival, so she had, in fact, been up and moving moments before her death.

Morgan returned to the victim. Anna's body was dry. Not a speck of water ran along her skin. The chair, however, was soaked from her presence. Her skin remained warm to the touch — too warm, even for the recently deceased.

Morgan opened the bathrobe. Dried blood was caked to her skin in thin streams from the three open wounds. Three shots matching the casings in the wall and the holes in the back cushion. Three. *How many did we hear outside? Were there three?*

The slamming of the back door pulled her away from the question. "Tell me you had better luck."

She refused to answer the question from Ben. She closed the bathrobe, then scanned the vicinity of the dead woman for something more. Tucked in the recliner beside Anna's corpse lay a small notepad and pen. Morgan lifted them loose and stood.

"Morgan?" Ben repeated.

"She was gone already. There was nothing I could do."

"Perfect."

"Nothing on your end?" she asked, reading his face for the answer.

"Less than nothing," he grumbled as Hendricks joined them in the living room. The federal agent rounded the sectional with ease, hands clenched tight to his sides.

"It was Henry Reed."

"You *think* it was Henry," Ben remarked.

"You have something to say, Agent Riley?" Hendricks shot back with a snarl.

"I just said it."

Hendricks cocked his fist. Ben stood with a smug grin across his face, waiting for the blow. Morgan cleared her throat. Her arms crossed her chest. "How about we not fight in front of the dead woman?"

Hendricks lowered his arm. His head fell and he paused. The agent crouched, and he slipped a glove over his hand as he reached beneath the coffee table. All eyes trailed his movements curiously. When his hand returned to view he was holding a revolver.

"How did you—?"

"A .45," Hendricks said.

"Serial number?"

"Looks like it's been defaced." He held it out to Morgan, who found an evidence bag in her pocket to catalog for later.

Ben rubbed his chin. "Who would—?"

"I don't see why we're debating what happened here," Hendricks said, ignoring his question. "Why do we care if we lost sight of the shooter? It was the kid."

"Her son?" Ben scoffed. "Henry shot his mother?"

Hendricks pointed to the gun. "You have another theory?"

"Than the one that makes the least amount of sense?"

Hendricks turned toward the deceased. "She sat there and took three to the chest. That means she knew her killer. Forensics will back that up, I guarantee it. Henry is capable of murder. We know this as well."

Ben held his tongue, a feat of strength Morgan had rarely seen from him. She waited for him to burst. Instead he sucked in a long breath and smiled. "Your thoughts, Agent Dunleavy?"

She nodded, the gun in full view before her. "Why shoot her?" Hendricks opened his mouth to respond and she waved him down. "Say it *is* Henry Reed for a second. He's been playing the part of a pyro or whatever for these fires you're investigating. So why does he decide to get up close and personal with mommy dearest?"

"Maybe she confronted him?" Hendricks said, reaching for something unseen. Intuition or something more, Morgan couldn't say for certain, having only known the man for less than twelve hours.

"Why don't we ask him first?" Ben interjected.

Morgan nodded. She passed along the note from the recliner. "I found this next to her."

The top sheet read: JEN-PAD.

"A new target?"

"Could be," Morgan answered.

"I'll call in more men," Hendricks said, pulling out his phone. "We can handle this on our end."

"Oh, I'm sure," Ben replied. He cut Hendricks off at the end of the couch. Hendricks attempted to work around the stubborn agent, then stopped in aggravation. Ben snatched the phone from the man and tossed it to the couch. "No, please. You're doing great so far. Definitely cut us out. You don't even know if Henry is your arsonist slash murderer. The only thing you know is that he's involved somehow."

"What are you saying?"

"I'm saying that if he isn't your killer, then there's a damn good chance he might be the next victim."

CHAPTER THIRTEEN

The day faded behind a wall of questions. Local PD arrived quickly to the scene. Ben let Morgan take the lead on bringing them up to date. Forensics entered the pistol into evidence. Ben stayed quiet while they worked. He ran through the details of the room in his mind. Anna Reed knew her attacker, that much was widely recognized. To Ben, it still failed to lock her son into the position of lead suspect, though everyone else involved pretended otherwise.

Maybe it motivated them, having someone to blame. It kept them focused on a single narrative instead of flailing for answers — which appeared to be fast becoming a DSA tradition.

Ben's silence seemed to unnerve Morgan more than his snark, though she remained professional in front of the other departments all working to put a dead woman to rest. When the questions finally ended, Ben left with Hendricks to follow their one and only lead from the scene.

By the time the pair arrived at Jen-Pad, dusk had settled over the city. Zac joined them. His anger over being locked in the bathroom for most of the day made for awkward conversation on their way to the facility.

Jen-Pad dealt in pharmaceuticals, a comparison not lost on any of them as they arrived. While Shur-Rite served as a corporation that bought formulas from competitors to market generic variations, Jen-Pad was at the forefront of research and development. Clinical trials ran within the ten-floor structure, their own marketing staff and customer service occupying separate floors from main operations.

A dour-looking security guard greeted them at the desk to

the right of the entrance. Along with a perpetual frown, he carried a clipboard and pen, the writing instrument providing background noise with its clicking.

"ID, please?"

Ben held back to make room for Hendricks at the desk. "Yours looks more professional."

Zac's glare burrowed into him like a pair of drills, and Hendricks offered his own distaste for the comment. "Are you joking?"

"Do you disagree?"

"It's fine. It's... you know what? I'm not doing this with you." Hendricks sighed then reached into his pocket. The guard took the badge in hand. His pen clicked incessantly while he reviewed the information.

After jotting down the relevant details, he passed the badge back to the waiting agent. Zac leaned close to Ben, jaw clenched.

"I can't believe you."

"What?"

"I put that badge together," Zac seethed.

"I know," Ben chided. "That's why I said it."

Hendricks cleared his throat. "Can we do this elsewhere?"

The guard clicked his pen louder. "That would be wonderful."

"Right," Ben muttered.

"You're looking for who, again?" the guard asked.

"Henry Reed," Zac answered. He opened his phone with a swipe and displayed an image on the screen. "I have a photo here."

"New kid," the guard grumbled. "Figures. I have to mark this down."

Hendricks rolled his eyes, unable to listen to the clicking any longer. His hand fell on the man's pen, a sharp scowl bearing down on the guard. "Which way?"

"Down the hall. Take a left. Janitorial staff is situated at the end."

Ben offered a silent thanks. Hendricks moved to the right of the extensive lobby while Zac trailed behind, phone still in hand. He swiped through options until settling on a single image.

"How about this for an enhancement to the badge?"

Ben took the phone. The DSA logo had been altered, the eagle more prominent and the American flag locked in the background.

"It doesn't matter, Zac," he said. "No one knows what the hell the DSA is anyway. Does your new design solve that little hiccup?"

"That's why *he's* here," Zac replied, pointing to Hendricks.

"Exactly," Ben said. He stopped and Zac followed suit. "Why are *you* here?"

"Are you still on that?" Zac snapped. "Is that why you ditched me this morning? And thank you oh so much for that one. Love spending my day in the bathroom."

"With what you eat I assumed that was standard procedure."

"What the hell is your problem?"

"I thought that was clear," Ben argued. "My problem is you. In the field."

"This is your concern right now?"

"One of many, yes. I'm very good at juggling lines of inquiry. And at juggling."

"I can't believe *either* of you are here," Hendricks interjected, his deep voice shattering their hushed tones. "Seriously, do you have any field experience at all?"

"The voice of reason," Zac whispered.

"Jury's still out on that one," Ben said. They started down the hall once more. "But a nice transition nonetheless. When it comes to approaching Henry we should be calm and rational."

"He's a killer," Hendricks said.

"One possibility," Ben shot back. "Or, he's not and we scare him off instead of finding out what the hell is going on. So let's approach this with a cool head and let him—"

They rounded the corner, a bank of elevators crowding the far wall. The janitorial supply room and staging area sat to the left, and a sign overhead clearly marked the area. To the right, outside the men's room, sat a large cart and mop bucket. Holding the mop along with a look of pure exhaustion was none other than Henry Reed.

"FBI!" Hendricks shouted, gun in hand. "FREEZE!"

The mop fell from his hands. The handle clattered against the spotless marble of the floor. It rolled toward the trio, the distraction less than a second, yet enough time for Henry to burst into a full run for the elevators.

Hendricks raced after him, Zac and Ben left in his imaginary dust.

"Great," Ben cursed.

Hendricks stopped halfway down the hall as their suspect slipped into an open elevator, the doors slow to close. The agent waved his arms in disbelief.

"Well? Come on!"

CHAPTER FOURTEEN

"Crap."

Henry jammed his thumb against the door control in the elevator, repeating the curse and the action in rapid succession while hoping for a favorable outcome. The elevator chimed over the rushing of feet down the corridor. When the sliding doors slammed together and the pulley began its ascent, Henry took a breath.

"What now?" It was a simple question without a response. A better one hung in the background. *What the hell was I thinking?* Coming to work, pretending normality when everything screamed at the change in his life, was the worst of a series of mistakes. Reginald Kane had died because of him. Nothing could wipe that stain on his soul clean. To be so arrogant as to believe he'd done the deed without the chance of reprisal, without the greatest consequence of all, was beyond ignorance.

So was running away in a panic. The sight of the gun, the mention of the FBI's involvement, forced Henry's brain to react without pause. Without a single thought as to what came next. About who would take care of his mother if he should be arrested or, given the mounting evidence against him, convicted for a man's brutal murder.

The cause of death, no doubt, remained an open question. How he killed Kane would top the interrogation. His answer ended any chance of a normal existence, of credulity as a member of the human race.

All, however, boiled down to his original query: *What do I do now?*

The elevator was a box to be switched off at any moment.

Taking it to the top was not a viable option in that regard. Henry hit the third-floor button just before the car passed by his intended destination and the elevator shook in response. The doors struggled from the shift. He ran between them before they finished opening.

The third floor of Jen-Pad opened to an immense space. Offices built out from the walls on either side ran the length of the floor. From the center, however, a series of partitions divided teams of customer-service agents and marketing departments. A four-pack of desks in one, ten more in another, all split by five-foot-high walls of metal interlocked into grand halls that twisted and turned worse than a corn maze.

Henry had made his first turn when a chime rang out from behind. Another elevator arrived and three pairs of pitter-pattering steps rushed along the floor. He couldn't look, couldn't take another breath. His fleeing feet drove him deeper into the maze.

"Where is he?" one asked, the voice a bellow in the empty expanse of the vacant area.

"There! He's there!"

Henry stopped. The out-of-place agent with the button down and double chin pointed in his direction, blowing his chances for a quick disappearing act.

Crap.

The glance back and his quick pace tripped him up. He drove headfirst into a nearby wall. The metal panel snapped, and it sent a shockwave rippling to the adjacent wall until they fell in a heap upon a row of desks. Computer components and keepsakes scattered under the debris.

Bob was going to be pissed in the morning. Henry, however, simply hoped to make it to see another hour let alone the dawn over the Chicago skyline.

He ran, leaving behind the destruction. His pursuers scurried closer and closer with each stride until at last he reached his destination.

The elevators were at the opposite side of the floor. The doors of the farthest to the left opened and Henry jumped in without delay. He mashed his thumb into the first-floor button. Then he collapsed in a heap in the corner, clutching his knees and tucking them close.

It was a quick trip. The doors clanged along their tracks, and a smile cracked the surface of the young man's face. Gripping the rail on the side of the car, Henry stood and stepped out. If he could reach the front entrance before the agents returned, and if by some miracle they hadn't bothered to leave someone on the street, then he could get clear for another night.

He needed another chance to figure out some way to survive after what he had done—if not for his own sake, then for his mother's. She had protected their secret for almost two decades and he'd managed to blow it to hell in a single act. He just prayed he wasn't too late to make things right for her.

Unfortunately, he was. Not because of extra manpower waiting in the lobby or beyond, but due to his own ignorance as to the layout of the building. The left bank of elevators didn't connect to the lobby. They skirted beneath the angled structure to a storage level for archived documents and equipment. A small hallway stretched in both directions from the elevator. Doors ran along the right-hand wall, each labeled for specific departments. All were closed.

"Oh no," he muttered, hands to his head in disbelief. Bob had shown him the layout, taken him through the tour only days earlier, yet somehow he'd failed to recall this small detail. Now his time had run out. The neighboring elevator rang, signaling its descent to his level.

Henry ran to the first door and turned the handle. Locked. The same result occurred with his second and third attempt. It wasn't until the end of the hall that the door gave way and he fell into the storage room within. He slammed the metal back into its frame and clicked the lock.

"Crap!"

Shelving surrounded him near the door, opening up to an empty space to the rear of the room. Near the ceiling was a sliding window barred from the outside. There was no door—just concrete walls and a sliver of freedom beyond them.

"What now?" Henry asked.

The agents were in the hall. Their muttering carried through the room as if they were right behind him. He was trapped; his life was over. Everything, every choice had led him here, and there was nothing left for him but to face the music and hope they understood.

"No," he whispered. He couldn't. Not with his mother still out there. Not with her life, no matter how little remained, at risk because of his mistake. He needed to fix it, but rushing headlong into the authorities wasn't the answer. Time was the key.

He blinked hard through pouring sweat; more dripped down his cheeks. His hands flattened against the concrete, pressing deeper and deeper into the wall. "Okay. Time for plan B."

CHAPTER FIFTEEN

Locked. Every door in the hall fought his pursuit of their suspect. Ben twisted the knob of the last door to the right. Hendricks worked his way along the opposite side. Both were quick and diligent, content with the silence between them.

If Hendricks hadn't rushed in, gun in hand, none of this would have been necessary. It would have been a simple matter to talk to Henry, one lost immediately by the overzealous agent. Suspect or not, their questions required a living body, not the target Hendricks had pinned to the kid.

"Anything?" Ben called. Hendricks shook his head. A curse slipped from Ben's lips. His head hit the door in frustration. Before he could pull away, his forehead settled along the metal frame. A sound whistled from the other side.

Wind.

"Here!" he yelled. "Over here!"

He took a step back and unleashed kick after kick against the shining knob. It finally snapped off, clattering along the ground. Unclasping his holster but never releasing the weapon, Ben slammed into the door and knocked it loose from the frame.

Cold greeted him, boxes and debris from the storage closet surrounding the entrance. He pushed away from the clutter to the open space at the rear of the room. Hendricks followed close, and the pair halted at the sight awaiting them.

"What the hell?" Hendricks muttered.

The back wall, a concrete slab running the entire length, was missing a chunk in the center. Not a clean cut, but a hole, dripping from the edges. It was large enough to allow a quick egress for a single individual.

Henry was gone.

"How?" Ben asked.

Hendricks pushed through. He carefully edged for the hole in the wall before clambering outside into the winter night. "Maybe we can ask a few more questions or, I don't know, go after him?"

Ben pointed to the wall; the glass from the barred window on top had melted and was dripping along the sides. "Yeah, great idea. Hendricks, we have no idea what this guy is capable of."

"Capable of?" Hendricks scoffed. "I've been telling you that the whole time. *He* burned Kane to death. What the hell does he care about a wall? He's on the run. If we catch him now—"

"He will panic," Ben interrupted. "He will panic, and you will end up all kinds of dead."

"Just me in this scenario?"

"Mostly you, yes."

The door slammed open. Both men drew their weapons on instinct as Zac staggered through the storage closet, cheeks flush and chest heaving. Noting the violence directed at him, Zac's hands shot up and he nearly fell back into the shelving lining the space.

"Again with the guns?" he shouted between gulps of air. Both men sighed and lowered their weapons. "What did I miss?"

Ben shoved his pistol back into the holster. "Your calling in the hundred-meter dash obviously."

Zac grimaced. He peered around with his hands to his hips. "So where is he?"

"The gaping hole is the only clue I can give."

"Enough!" Hendricks bellowed from outside. "Enough with the damn jokes. Enough with wasting our time. I'm going after him."

"Hendricks…"

"No!" the agent snapped. "I've had it with your inability to see what's in front of you. Henry Reed is our only lead, my only lead, with these fires—and with these deaths. He's where your head should be at instead of dicking around and making everyone else miserable."

"You're wrong."

Hendricks shook his head. "I'm not. You coming or not?"

Ben stepped into the night air, hand grazing the warm concrete, and stopped. He returned to the confines of the storage room. "You go ahead."

"Just like that?"

"Ben, you can't let him… he doesn't mean it, Hendricks," Zac said, stumbling through his words. He wasn't wrong. They needed Hendricks, his authority as their local contact, to continue their work on the case. He legitimized them. None of that mattered. What truly concerned Zac, as much as it worried Ben, was how pissed off Morgan would be with his decision.

Ben shrugged. "Good luck, Hendricks."

"Unbelievable," the federal agent grumbled. "So glad to have you as backup on this case. Damn DSA."

"Happy to help," Ben said with a salute. Hendricks flipped him off, then bolted out of sight. The shadows swallowed every last trace of the man.

The howling wind flowed through the space, cooling the wall. Ben's hand ran the length as he noted the corrosion, the pieces of slab left in the wake of Henry's escape.

Behind him, Zac cleared his throat. "You're really letting him go out there without backup?"

"And leave you here all by your lonesome?" Ben asked with a smile. "Perish the thought."

"My hero." Zac handed Ben a pair of gloves, then slipped on his own. He examined the sheared glass overhead, following the trail along the left ridge. "So how did Henry—?"

"Exactly."

"Is this why you let Hendricks go?"

Ben nodded. "Did you hear an explosion of any kind? See a device that could have done this in the minute he might have had before the door came down? Hendricks is chasing a man, a run-of-the-mill pyro that finally crossed the line to murder, but I think there's more going on with Mr. Henry Reed than we know."

Zac offered a nod in agreement, and returned to the wall. He snapped images of the scene with his camera. Morgan would want them right away. "You think Hendricks knows more than he's saying?"

Zac's question mirrored his own. Hendricks hadn't commented on the wall, had never glanced at the edges of the concrete or searched the confines of the room for debris from an explosive device. He had charged ahead with one thing on his mind: his tunnel vision for a suspect and an arrest to close the case.

It was almost as if he needed the young man for another reason altogether.

"If he does," Ben started, the unexplained melted wall at his fingertips, "then it's time to stop playing catch up and start coming up with some answers. Hopefully it's not too late."

CHAPTER SIXTEEN

A janitor welcomed Morgan to the medical examiner's office. His jangling keys accompanied the buzzing lights of the hall in providing background music to their walk through the building. He said barely a word, and she offered nothing in return. Their shared silence was peaceful compared to the rest of her day.

The police had joined the crime scene at the Reed home soon after being called. After their initial questioning, Morgan had departed for the front stoop, unwilling to spend another moment with the dead woman inside. There would be time enough for that later, and she had done her tour with the dead already.

They reminded her of the shortcomings that had led to her recruitment to the DSA: the mistakes constantly following her like a shadow. Still, the dead clung tight to her, they filled her waking world. She was always cognizant of their former lives — those better spent than the one she had thrown away and the one she failed to live with each passing day.

That emptiness surrounded her. She struggled to connect and fought to build a bridge with anyone. It was worse since Bellbrook, her instinct to actively seek the solitude of the job rather than work with others.

So lost in thought, Morgan almost barreled through the janitor, who stopped short near the end of the corridor. A woman slipped through a pair of doors. She wore uncomfortable heels and a crooked smile. Thick glasses slid down her nose; a thin strand of thread had been looped around her neck to keep them from crashing to the floor. Her petite frame matched her delicate fingers, extended in greeting.

"Diane Phelps," the woman said. "You're here about the

body?"

"That's right," Morgan replied, taking her hand. With a nod, the lone member of the cleanup crew left her to the newcomer. "Morgan Dunleavy."

"Thanks for waiting." Diane moved for the autopsy suite taking up the back half of the building. "Protocol in these matters, I'm afraid."

"I understand."

"Come on back. I was just restarting the digital recorder. Thing's been buggy all day."

The double doors opened to the morgue. Dingy walls covered in compartments surrounded the pair on both sides. Recording equipment, computer analysis, and testing gear occupied much of the interior to the front. It provided a buffer to the dangling spotlights hovering over the slabs that decorated the theatre. Two bodies rested on the closest tables, the others sparkling from a recent cleaning.

Phelps almost tripped, her heels a detriment more than a fashion statement. Morgan reached for her with each clumsy step, but the medical examiner managed to correct her descent until she was finally able to rest a hand on a nearby slab for stability.

She kicked off the shoes the moment the double doors closed. "Thank God."

"Dress code requirement?"

"Unspoken one," Diane muttered as she rubbed her left foot. "You wouldn't think it would be a big deal to dress down for the dead, but then you get your quarterly review and there it is, listed next to workplace etiquette."

Morgan fell silent, unsure what to say. Diane read her trepidation with a smile and waved her to the waiting work ahead, allowing the agent to breathe once again.

Anna Reed's naked form, pale skin dotted by three entry wounds to her chest, rested in complete distinction compared to the mangled mess of Reginald Kane's remains. As Diane walked over to the newcomer of their impromptu party, Morgan paused at the first.

"Has there been any clear sign of —"

Diane stopped her, tapping the microphone hanging over Anna's body. It connected to the laptop on the desk beside the slabs, the recording software primed and ready. "Sorry, one sec," Diane said, clicking the button. "Coroner Phelps' report on the body of Anna Reed. Second recording due to technical glitch. I'm joined by Agent Morgan Dunleavy with the... What organization was it again?"

"FBI," Morgan answered with a disarming grin. It helped mask her contempt for having to utilize outside help in these situations. Work, however, trumped her pride on the issue, and she rolled with it as best as she could. "A consultant for the agency."

"Right," Diane said without a second glance. "As previously noted—"

"I hate to interrupt again."

Diane let go of the microphone, head falling to her chest. Her glasses slipped loose and dangled beneath until she caught them. "But you will anyway."

"I was hoping to start with Kane."

Diane hesitated, glasses positioned tight, though they had already started their slow descent. "All right," she started. She slowly rounded the slab to their second dance partner of the evening. "I took tissue samples, but I couldn't make heads or tails of what could have done this to him."

"*Who* could have, you mean."

"I'm sorry?"

Morgan tore loose some gloves from a nearby shelf and snapped them into position. Taking the opposite side to her companion, she quickly sifted through the bone matter yet to be cleaned for the proper piece. Lifting the ulna, she examined it before showing the evidence to the waiting coroner.

"Looks like there's been further degradation since being moved, but take a peek."

Diane took the bone, eyes widening at the sight. "Is that a handprint? That... that is awesome."

"Awesome?"

"Amazing? Spectacular? Sensational?" the excited woman rambled. "That makes more sense considering..." She placed the bone carefully along the slab before breaking out in a jog for the lab. "Over here, over here."

Morgan stopped short of the waiting microscope. A thin slide clicked into place at the base and Diane moved aside for her colleague.

"What did you find?"

"Samples taken off the deceased," Diane explained. "I found polymers in the flesh."

"Synthetic? Like a glove of some kind?"

Diane shook her head. "Not the case here, no. These are organic."

Morgan leaned close, focusing the lens on the item in question. Small cells danced on the slide. "Skin? From the killer?"

"Not just skin," the exuberant medical examiner said. "It's much denser than any skin I've ever seen. The structure of the cells is more layered than the average Jack and Jill. I was about to send these on for further testing but, well..."

A pile of waiting envelopes rested at the edge of the makeshift lab. It appeared the office couldn't handle their current workload. The system seemed as close to the positive side of inefficient as legally acceptable.

Morgan left the slide behind for the waiting body. "And Kane himself?"

"Lit up like a Menorah," Diane said. "But how? That I haven't quite figured out. Nothing on the spectrum, and I ran the gamut with tests. Odorless. Chemically induced. Poison of some kind. Nada. Just fwoosh."

"Fwoosh?"

"Fwoosh." Diane nodded. Her hands acted out the sound for her. "Big time fwooshing."

"Leaving us with Anna Reed."

"Yes. Right." The medical examiner cleared her throat, the recording waiting for her prompt. "Back to our regularly scheduled autopsy. Now, as noted in my first recording, Anna Reed suffered three gunshot wounds. All at close range, and all to the thoracic cavity."

A clear sign of death. An open-and-shut case, yet everything screamed at Morgan to ask for more information. She was missing something, some vital clue to make sense of what surrounded the mystery of the victim's son and the deaths that seemed to follow him.

Diane lifted her scalpel. "I have begun the 'Y' incision to investigate the damage from the bullets."

Morgan covered the microphone slightly. "Has the tox screen

been completed?"

"Not yet, though I'm not expecting much. Looks pretty clear-cut. Three shots and here we go, right? Not like our Kentucky Fried executive over there."

"Maybe."

Diane paused. "Maybe?"

"There was something about the scene. I don't know exactly..."

"Not sure what I can tell you. You're the investigator."

"Should we be talking like this with the recording going?" Morgan dropped her hand from the microphone.

"I edit it afterward," she said. "I usually have a few points to add so I go through and clean up the report. Mostly, it's me deleting all the F-bombs I tend to drop. I'm trying to be better about that kind of thing."

"That's... good."

Diane read the wary glance. "Right. Here we—"

Morgan snapped her fingers. "Body temperature."

"What?" the exasperated coroner asked.

"At the crime scene. She was warm."

"She had just been shot."

"I'm aware of that."

"Then what?"

"It was more than warm. She was... I don't know, radiating heat or something. Hot, even. What was her temp when she arrived?"

Diane lowered the scalpel and proceeded to the foot of the slab. Her initial findings ran along the clipboard and she scanned the results. "Nothing unusual. A steady drop of 1.5 degrees per hour since time of death. Rigor mortis set in per usual as well."

Morgan backed off, content with the findings for the moment. She needed the woman to complete her work while she was present and had a feeling she was close to being shown the door for her questioning attitude.

Diane lifted the scalpel once more. The silence allowed her to complete the incision along the woman's chest and down her abdomen. "Whoa."

"What?"

"I have completed the incision," she stated for the recording.

"The bones appear to be calloused along the rib cage. Almost like—"

"Scar tissue?" Morgan interjected, leaning close. "Sorry."

"Yes. Scar tissue."

That wasn't possible. Adhesions occurred after a significant injury or surgery. There were no signs present on the woman's skin. No reason for scar tissue to form, and certainly not to that degree. Morgan took a step away from the body, pointing suddenly to Anna Reed's forehead.

"Doctor?" she called. "Sweat."

"What are you—?" Diane stopped, following Morgan to the beads forming along the dead woman's brow.

"Check her temperature again. Your victim appears to be sweating."

"Incredible," Diane said. She shook her head, then returned to the open cavity at her center. "Give me one second here. I'm removing the rib cage for a closer look."

They snapped under the pressure and the almost jubilant examiner removed the woman's ribs. She placed them in the waiting receptacle near the table. Light from above beamed into the open chest cavity. Diane's eyes widened at the sight inside. Not a single vital organ lay exposed. Every anatomy lesson fell away at the sight of the dead woman.

"What is it?" Morgan asked.

"Best guess?" Diane said. "More scar tissue. Like a protective sheath over her organs. Every single one."

"Why would there be—"

"I've never seen anything like this," Diane interrupted, unable to contain her excitement any longer. "I have to call the lab and get a rush on that tox screen. Her organs, while not able to fight off the impact of the bullets, appear to have been cocooned from the heat her own body seems to be generating."

Diane removed the right lung, careful not to disturb the shell concealing the organ. In the center was a small bullet hole, which had cut straight through the tissue protecting Anna throughout her body.

"Hand me that scale," Diane commanded. "I am going to write a paper on this shi—sorry."

Morgan cleared some space next to the laptop and placed the scale down. The lung clanged against the metal basin. "Doctor?"

"Let's see here," Diane continued. "Right lung of the subject weighs—"

"Phelps!" Morgan shouted. "Back up!"

"What are you...?" She turned from the scale and took a step away from the slab. Sweat poured like a stream along Anna's skin. In an instant, heat billowed from the deceased, building until the victim burst into flames from head to toe.

"HOLY!" Diane jumped, rushing away from the body to join Morgan in the relative safety of the lab. The flames rose a foot off the body, never extending any farther, but warming the entire room.

"How?" Morgan whispered. Ben's theory from the previous night echoed in her thoughts. "I mean... Is this what I think it is?"

"It can't be. It's physically impossible. A myth."

"She's on fire, Doctor Phelps."

"But to call it..." She shook her head. "I can't even say it."

"Spontaneous combustion."

"Hoax. Always a hoax."

Morgan extended her hand over the flames. "Can you feel that? It's controlled. How is that possible?"

"Jesus Christ," the doctor said. She offered the sign of the cross immediately. She removed her glasses, the fire dancing in her eyes. "She's turning her radiant heat into an expendable energy source."

"Try and hold back on that paper, Doc."

Diane grinned. "I feel like toasting marshmallows."

They stared in awe, time fading behind their curiosity. Moments slipped away, and then as mysteriously as they started, the flames waned, receding along the pale skin of Anna Reed. The deceased appeared untouched, unfazed by the sudden desire to turn into a campfire. Morgan inched closer. Her fingers glided along the slab until they came to rest along the woman's ankle.

"Hey!" Diane yelled. "Don't touch her after—"

"She's cold," Morgan exhaled. "Like ice."

Diane joined her. "Incredible."

Morgan pointed to the microphone, following the setup bridging from the laptop to cameras in the corner. "You were recording this?"

"Yeah?" Diane took a second to process the statement. Her face lit up. "Yes!"

Morgan smiled. "There isn't a mark on her."

"The scar tissue," Diane said. "It's like a buffer."

Morgan nodded. "Some form of protection. And her skin—"

"Released the heat without absorbing any of it. How does that—?"

The lights dimmed, blinking repeatedly before falling away. Darkness enveloped the room.

"What the hell?"

"Come on," Diane grumbled. "Why does this always happen?"

"Power outage?"

Diane clambered for the front of the room. "Dammit. City is lousy with brownouts. I'll check with Mel out front and… what the hell?"

"Phelps?"

The once boisterous coroner fell silent. She slipped from the edge of the table and smashed to the ground. Morgan rushed to her side.

"Diane!" She checked the fallen woman's pulse. Her heart slowed to a crawl, but it still beat. As her fingers danced along Diane's artery Morgan noticed a small object embedded in the skin. "What is—?"

A whisper of air cut across the room and slapped against her side. Pain shot along her back. Her tongue was instantly numb. Distant fingers pulled at the point of impact until at last stumbling on the object. She held it close, dots darkening her vision, but she was able to glimpse the item clearly for a split second.

A dart.

It fell, clattering in front of her along the tile. She joined the tranquilizer a second later as her forehead slammed against the tile. Her body no longer answered her commands. As she lay paralyzed against the cold ground, she noted the arrival of three shadows to the room. Dressed in black and wearing goggles, they worked seamlessly through the morgue.

"Move it," one said in a low whisper.

The second nodded, pointing across the room. "Recordings and the bodies. Be sure to grab those samples as well. Nothing stays."

"And these two?" their third companion asked.

"He said to leave them for now. Hopefully they get the message."

Who? Morgan fought to ask. Her tongue lolled from her lips, numb like the rest of her body. She struggled to stay conscious, to hear everything, but the shadows grew thicker, spiraling around her.

"Where is he anyway?"

"He's on his way to the rendezvous. Tracking our target still."

Another tapped his wrist. "We're on the clock. Sixty seconds before security is alerted."

Their work completed, the trio rushed for the door. *Wait...* Morgan shouted in her thoughts, her vision failing. Pain overtook her and the darkness was complete.

Wait...

CHAPTER SEVENTEEN

The morning brought little in the way of light. There was gray and more gray in the offing, clouds rushing in with another winter storm on the horizon. Traffic, the only constant in the landscape, rushed through downtown and took over all avenues of travel.

Ben yawned, the iced coffee a compromise that upset his stomach but was required for the early start. Zac had woken him from his troubled sleep. Dreams of fire kept full-on rest at bay, his exhaustion the only thing keeping his eyes closed for a time.

Sleep had to wait, however. Zac had found Henry Reed, or at least a possible connection to their suspect. No answer had come from Morgan's room or from her phone when they went to bring her up to speed. She had yet to inform them about her trip to the medical examiner's office. Zac's concerns, while noted, did nothing to halt Ben's desire to find some form of answer. A message was left, and they continued their hunt for the mysterious young man at the heart of their mystery.

Their cab ride ended at a storage unit on the Upper West Side. The manager gave them access without question, the words *federal* and *agent* enough to send the greasy-haired man racing for the keys.

The unit itself held no significance, much to Ben's dissatisfaction. All he asked for was a clear sign of guilt or innocence over the matter of two deaths. Books lined a small desk in the corner, yet none contained titles like HOW I KILLED REGINALD KANE or HERE IS MY AIRTIGHT ALIBI FOR THE MURDER OF MY MOTHER. Those would have been helpful, to say the least.

Henry's storage unit *did* offer a glimpse at the kid's life. Unlike the Reed home, which was spartan in regard to his belongings, this home away from home contained many of the trappings of youth. Toys, stuffed animals, high school yearbooks, and the like sat in stacked boxes along the right-hand wall. A couch rested in the back, a pillow and blanket making a clear case as to where Henry hid when required.

"Anyone here?" a voice called from outside.

Ben peered around the corner. "Come on in, Morgan."

Bleary-eyed and wearing a large bandage along her forehead, Morgan entered the confined space. "Cozy."

Zac lowered the books on the desk. His excitement turned to concern at the woman's arrival. "What the hell happened to you?"

Morgan winced, holding tight to her head. "We'll get there."

"How about right now?" he pressed.

"I said—"

Ben cut her off. "We'll get there, Zac. What did you find?"

Zac hesitated, wanting to force the issue. Relenting, he returned to the books. "Well, he likes to read."

"Astute observation."

"Seriously though," he continued. "This is some heavy reading for a kid just out of high school. Over-my-head-level stuff."

"So humble," Ben said.

Zac shrugged. "I keep it in check."

Morgan took the books from him. She scanned the titles methodically. "*Properties of Heat*? *Thermodynamics*? What is this *Reiki*—?"

"At least there are pictures." Ben glanced at the text as she flipped through the pages.

Morgan dropped the books along the desk and paced the small unit. Boxes were opened, all of them less than useful to their investigation. She collapsed on the couch.

"Morgan…"

"Where is Hendricks?"

Zac turned away, Ben catching his unease. "No idea. He took off last night. Hasn't checked in since."

"So we're here without authorization?"

"He was stonewalling us," Ben said, then stopped and let out a soft sigh. "I'll call later and ask, okay? I'm tired of playing 'Follow the Fed.'"

He waited for the screaming to begin. The reaction had built since his arrival on the case, threatening to erupt from her being every time he opened his mouth. Instead, she sucked in a hard breath and let it out slowly.

"That's fine."

"It is?"

"Better he's not here for this," Morgan said.

"What did the autopsy reveal?" Ben asked.

"Things I have a hard time believing, except they were right in my face."

Zac sat on the edge of the couch. "What was it?"

"Anna Reed's body," Morgan said, drawing out each word in hesitation. "It combusted."

"What?" Ben exclaimed. "How?"

"No idea." Her hands clamped in front of her. "Her internal temperature kept climbing during the autopsy until—" Her hands mimicked an explosion, spreading wide before her.

Zac leaned close. "Is that where the bruise came from?"

"No," she said, grazing the bandage. "This happened after."

"So her body just..."

"That's the thing. She should have been ash or badly scarred. Some kind of evidence that she lit up like a—"

"Human Torch?"

She grimaced. "We talked about that. But, yes. Just like that, and then nothing."

Ben huffed. "She was fine?"

Her eyes thinned. "Outside of the whole being dead thing? Yes."

The pair fell silent and shared a cold look. Morgan stood, cutting between them.

"Okay," she said. "Why are you two acting like this isn't the weirdest thing you've seen in the last twelve hours?"

Ben nodded to Zac. "Show her."

The tech handed over his phone. He guided her to a series of images captured the previous night in the lower level of Jen-Pad. Her eyes widened at the sheared-away glass and melted concrete displayed on the screen.

"How?"

"We're still figuring it out, but I'd say mother and son share some common traits."

"She passed it on to him," Morgan muttered.

"Passed on what, exactly?"

"I'm not sure," she said. "You need an external ignition source to create effects like this as well as the tools necessary to control them. Anna and Henry don't."

"They can channel heat."

"Lots of it."

Ben shook his head. "Did you get anything else from the autopsy? Something that might help us?"

She closed her eyes, hand to her forehead. Zac reached for her, though she pulled away.

"Hey," he called. "What happened last night?"

"One minute, I'm watching Anna Reed perform her best campfire scene, and then…" Hands to her hips she let out a groan of frustration. "Someone took the body and all the physical evidence."

"What?"

"The lights went out; I tried to see what was going on, and then?" She lifted her bandage to show the bruise spread along her brow. "I got lucky. Just a bad fall from the paralyzing agent in the dart."

"The medical examiner?"

"Still out of it," Morgan replied. "Bad reaction to the tranquilizer they used on us. That's what I was told, anyway."

"Morgan, are you—?"

"Pissed is all, Zac," she answered. "Really."

"We'll find her."

Morgan shook her head. "I shouldn't have lost her."

"Morgan—" Ben started, then stopped.

"We have questions that need answering. Let's get some answers."

"Right," Zac said. His frantic pace through the unit picked up. "Like why would Henry do this? Why shoot his own mother? And then, what, steal her body so we couldn't learn what he is? Does that make any sense? Again, why shoot someone when you could just scorch them?"

Ben winced. "We're not calling it that."

"Come on, Riley," Zac said. "I'm serious."

"Relax, Zac," Morgan said with a smirk. "They're all good

questions."

"And Henry didn't kill his mother," Ben noted.

Morgan's brow furrowed. "How do you—"

"The angle of the shots came from someone taller than our Mr. Reed," Ben continued. "Also, we only heard two shots outside, but she took three to the chest."

"We did?"

Ben nodded. "We did."

They moved for the exit and Zac pulled the overhead door to the floor. The lock clanged into position, keys dangling in the tech's hand. He caught up and passed them to Ben.

"So if he didn't kill his mother—"

"It stands to reason he didn't knock you out to steal her body and that he isn't the driving force of these attacks either."

"Then who is?" Zac asked.

Ben smiled. "I know someone we should ask."

"Yeah, right," Morgan huffed. "All we have to do is find Mr. Reed."

CHAPTER EIGHTEEN

The storage unit had been meant to be a safe place, somewhere unseen, unknown to the world. It was a refuge for Henry, his destination of choice to be alone, to contemplate life and the cruel curse that lay at his feet.

He had spent the night running, afraid to pause, terrified of looking back for some sign of pursuit. Henry had raced through the streets, the winding alleys, and the red-light district around Murray Hill until finally coming to rest at the park. No sirens blared nearby. No hurried footfalls chased after him in the darkness—only the silence condemning his actions. The dawn couldn't come soon enough and when it had finally arrived, it brought a hope unfelt since the Shur-Rite Building.

He had needed time, to think, to plan, to understand how things had spiraled so completely out of control. There was only one place for such a feat and it meant forgetting about his mother's worry. Henry had taken care to keep the storage unit a secret. He'd paid cash, face-to-face, leaving nothing to connect him to his refuge. It was not his only secret, though it ranked as his best kept.

Yet somehow they'd found him as easily as they had at Jen-Pad. The agents, two of whom he recognized from Jen-Pad, stepped out of the storage unit. They closed the heavy door, locking up as if they had never been there in the first place. They knew about it, infiltrating every facet of his life.

"Oh, no," he muttered. His hand slammed against his forehead and he stepped deeper into the alley across from the storage facility to avoid being spotted. If they had found out about the unit and about Jen-Pad, there was little doubt they had visited his mother.

All his concern broke through the surface. All his attempts to keep her safe and out of the affair had failed. His phone was in his hand the next instant, the number programmed and saved in the top recall spot.

What was there to say to her? What *could* be said to make sense of what he had done, the act of murder in self-defense adding up to little more than murder no matter how he spun the narrative. His mother required rest. He offered her nothing of the sort.

How had they known? How had they found him? The phone, poised in his hand, gleamed under the morning light. Of course. *His phone.* How else would they track his movements? How else could they have found the unit except through the device glued to his side at all times?

Henry held tight to a nearby brick wall. He reached back, the phone against his palm. As he brought it up to the thick edifice the device blared, echoing through the alley.

He answered the call, "Hello?"

"We need you to come in, Henry," the voice on the other end of the line said. "Time to stop running."

Henry held the phone back from his ear for a long moment. He recognized the voice, the hard edge to every word. Where he'd heard it before he couldn't say — however, it chilled him.

"Who is this?" he asked, swallowing his nerves.

"The situation —"

Henry scoffed. "Situation? Is that what this is?"

"I can help you, Henry."

"With what? I have federal agents at my storage unit! I've got people chasing me because of a package I never should have opened!"

"They aren't federal agents."

Henry settled against the cold wall of the alley. "Wow. That's what you lead with? Like it matters!"

"Henry," the voice continued. Irritation crept in the voice. The hardened tone sharpened with each breath. "I understand what you're going through, but I need you to —"

"I'll stop you there," Henry interrupted, hand in the air as if the man were sitting across from him. "If your next words were going to be calm and down, consider them ignored. I should just talk to them. That's what I've been thinking about ever since last night. I should never have run. I can explain what happened and we can—"

"Excuse me?" Irritation disappeared, quickly replaced by anger.

Henry stood to pace the trash-infested concrete. "No, listen. I can talk to them. Whoever they are. I can explain what happened. They'll have to understand."

"They won't." There was no doubt in the man's gravelly voice.

"You don't know that. You don't know what they'll—"

"They don't care about Shur-Rite," the voice snapped. "They don't care about Kane or any of it. Henry, they killed your mother."

"What?" Henry's feet gave way and his knees slammed against the ground. "What did you say?"

"She's dead. They shot her. Now they want you."

She's dead. It hollowed out his heart and Henry fully collapsed along the floor of the debris-filled alley. His mother was dead and there was no fighting the admission. Maybe it was why he hadn't been able to call her during his flight from the law. Like he'd already known somehow and had chosen to bury that loss rather than deal with it at the time.

"When?" he said, struggling against his grief.

"I'm sorry, Henry. We did everything—"

"No," the young man shot back. The words meant nothing coming from the voice, his tone showing no sign of sympathy at his plight. "Don't give me the company line. Not after everything. Was it you? Asking my mother to do these things? Was it you?"

"Henry—"

"Tell me!"

Traffic roared behind him and Henry scurried to his feet to hide deeper in the shadows against the rising light of day. Everything faded, even the sound of his tears crashing down his cheeks as he swiped them away.

"She served her country well," the voice replied. "She volunteered to work with our organization in exchange for protection. Anna was a patriot and deserved better."

What had she done? What had she been asked to do in service of some faceless government unable to fulfill their end of the deal? The lack of answers shocked him back to reality. How far had she fallen? How many Reginald Kanes were in *her* past?

"I want... I want to see her," Henry stammered. "I don't... I need to see her!"

"That's fine," the voice replied without pause. "Come in and we can make that happen."

"No."

"Henry," the man repeated. "Come in and we can—"

"Get me killed too? Pass." Henry dropped the phone and smashed it under his heel. The voice offered nothing but pain, and he had heard enough. There were no answers, only the truth about his mother.

The news of her loss tore at him. He had hidden to keep her safe, to give her a chance to live out her remaining days in peace. Instead, his help had killed her just as surely as if he'd pulled the trigger himself.

Sobbing uncontrollably, Henry covered his face with his hands. His tears ran hot against his frozen skin and he fought to keep them in check.

They had killed her, the agents leaving the storage unit. They had taken away his chance to be with her at the end, to let her go peacefully from this world, from a life that had been anything but.

Why? The question remained, and no answer from the spook on the phone had been forthcoming. He needed to find his own answers. Not by hiding. Not by thinking.

It was time for a new approach.

It was time to act.

CHAPTER NINETEEN

Lincoln reached the library overlooking Phoenix Park in downtown Lexington by mid-afternoon. The crowd within the five-story structure was limited. Few people milled about the rotunda, and a lone pair snapped photos of the ceiling clock contained within like a tourist attraction. Staffers worked to clean shelves and build up the entertainment areas, likely hoping to bring in more bodies over the approaching holiday break.

The focused soldier shuffled in without a sound. His presence brought enough attention. Eyes tracked his movements to the second floor and the specialized Kentucky Room. When the third white employee asked if he needed any assistance, Lincoln snapped.

"I'm good. If I want your help with something," Lincoln spat, while clenching his fist, "I'll ask."

The wary staffer backed away without another word, but the gaze remained. Lincoln almost forgot where he was in the country, a slip that tended to occur when in constant motion with the work of the DSA. Unfortunately, the people around him always managed to remind him and he realized what little progress had been made over the centuries.

Some battles truly were never-ending.

The Kentucky Room was a specialized collection containing local historical resources as well as census information for the state. Lincoln referred to the images tucked in his pocket to track the camera positions used to capture the image of the Witness only two days earlier. Two more visits had occurred over the course of the last week. Three separate trips to this room, all for some unknown reason.

Tracking the movements carried over by the photos taken at each circumstance, Lincoln shifted carefully about the room. The gaze from those within the space as well as those passing by was now completely justified, as he appeared to be part of a hazing ritual rather than a government agent tracking down a suspect.

Each image marked the man at a singular shelf. Lincoln stopped in front of the display, imagining the Witness present and standing before the rows of manuscripts. Tracking the cameras in the area, Lincoln realized their slow progression across the room. The Witness would have been standing in the same position for almost a full minute in order to be picked up at the exact spot captured in each image from the past month.

The Witness deliberately waited for the cameras to catch him there for the specific purpose of showcasing a single book from the collection. Why? Why would a man so careful about his identity, so paranoid about being seen as to hide behind opaque lenses, commit to exposing this simple deed?

Lincoln tracked the shelves until he found the desired book. Like most of the room, the shelf carried extensive histories of prominent Kentucky families. It labeled them in alphabetical order, some dating back centuries, while others were relatively fresh from the presses.

It wasn't until his hand fell against the decorated spine, one with gold trim along the top and bottom, that Lincoln understood the significance behind the book. A stylized version of the letter E occupied the center of the thick tome and Lincoln required two hands to steady the pages.

THE ENGERS LINE OF AMERICAN PATRIOTS
ARTHUR TO MORRISON

"It can't be..." Lincoln muttered. Pages spun from his finger, unable to move fast enough to keep pace with his spiraling thoughts. When he hit the end of the lengthy document depicting the history of one of the most provincial families in Kentucky, a small slip of paper fell from the binding. The single sheet floated through the air, dipping back and forth in the bleary-eyed soldier's line of sight before skidding along the decorative flooring.

Morrison Engers stared at him from the book—Senator Morrison Engers. For Lincoln, no reading was required to know the man. In his six years of service, as the head of his Secret Service detail, he had learned everything about Morrison.

How could the Witness know about him?

Lincoln closed the book. Careful hands slipped the massive tome back into place on the shelf. It was the least he could do after what had happened.

Slowly, agonizing over every inch, Lincoln crouched to retrieve the vital document at his feet. He opened it. His eyes wandered through the room for privacy and surprised to find some given by those still wandering the building. Thick black ink marked the page. Three lines—that was it. Three lines slammed into Lincoln harder than the bullet through his bicep, deeper than his heartache over losing Ruth and so many more over the course of his life.

DES MOINES

THREE DAYS

YOU KNOW WHERE

Impossible. The whole affair had been a secret; the inquiry following the Des Moines event had been classified from public view. Lincoln's name didn't even make it into the final report, his guilt enough to warrant his dismissal without the need for the press to condemn him. Yet somehow the Witness knew everything. From the smallest detail to the most obvious, all was within reach for the man who controlled the agenda—and Lincoln's next move.

CHAPTER TWENTY

The day did not go well. It faded quickly behind a blur of searching and unraveling the life of Henry Reed. Unfortunately, their target was a rarity in the modern age: a kid hidden from a social-media-laced culture of self-involvement. Off the grid—the term striking Ben as ludicrous—fit their suspect perfectly and offered them a complete lack of leads.

They started at the Reed home, where they located a late delivery in the trash, the box empty save for a note directing the contents to be sent along to the Shur-Rite Building, which made a clear case for Henry's presence at Reginald Kane's demise. The money found in the back of his closet solidified motive in their eyes.

Jen-Pad made the list as well. Interviews with his current supervisor, the shocked Bob Patterson, pointed to a bright and enthusiastic employee in Mr. Reed with none of the violent tendencies being built up by their investigation.

Night approached, the day wasted to interviews and little else. Compromise fell away and frustration mounted. Most came from the fairer sex, though Zac's continual sugar crashes didn't help matters either. With the moon fighting through the clouds and a break in the endless winter storm, they returned to the storage unit that had started their day.

Ben paced the end of the row containing Henry's home away from home. His hands were tucked deep into his pockets to keep from playing with his earpiece or his bloodstained tie. Morgan took a bench outside the property, staying within sight, but able to monitor the traffic rushing from downtown.

He didn't need to see her, however, to hear the growing rage beneath every scoff, the anger left with each antagonizing question. Two hours and Ben was ready to call the whole thing off, if only for a moment of peace.

"He's not coming back here," Morgan said, her deep voice cutting off his thoughts. It matched her previous two statements of the last hour, each one a biting commentary over his judgment, though he had let them slide. "Did you hear me?"

"He might," Ben said, jaw clenched. "Where else would he go?"

"Anywhere outside Chicago would be my guess."

Ben's fists squeezed inside his pockets. "Which we're tracking via our walking, talking internet in the car."

"Where we should be too," she replied. She took a long, satisfying sip of her coffee before wrapping in close along the bench.

"I'm open to suggestions." He grimaced at the statement. All his efforts to curb his tongue failed, and each was returned with nothing more than complaints and anger. She did everything she could to be the opposite, to carry a massive chip on her shoulder — to blast and condemn those around her instead of working with them to solve the case.

"Hell, I don't know. Another apartment? A friend's house? A former co-worker? He might have a site he uses to lay low between targets."

"Targets?" Ben laughed. "You're sounding like Hendricks."

"Where *is* Hendricks?"

Ben bit his lip. They had waited all day to hear from the man. Hendricks was in the wind and Ben wasn't sure whether or not he caught up to their suspect and met his end or if he was simply pissed off at their working relationship.

He suspected the latter, though the former nagged at his guilt over letting the situation devolve the way it had at Jen-Pad. Something, however, convinced Ben it had been the right move at the time.

"You call him?" Ben asked.

"No answer. Left a message." Another sip passed through the radio. "Shouldn't he be here suffering through this weather with us?"

"Yeah," Ben said. "He's not returning my calls either."

The lie ate at him, but it kept her from pressing the issue. It was the last thing he wanted. More than anything, he wanted to trust Morgan. With everything bearing down on him since the end of his former life in Buffalo and his desire to rectify that situation, Ben needed someone to trust.

His apartment was bugged. He was being followed by government goons. Even Zac's presence on the case did nothing to allay his concerns—the tech's excuses flimsy at best. There was no one left to trust. Yet he continued to turn to Morgan for a chance to build something more. To be a friend.

A partner.

"Morgan," he called.

"Riley."

"How old is your nephew?"

Her head lowered, the coffee resting at her side. Morgan shook her head. "Ten more minutes and I say we move on. Maybe head in for the night and pick up the trail in the morning."

"You really think Henry is doing this all on his own?"

"He could be," she said, her words sharp against his eardrum.

"Why?" he asked. "There is nothing in his background. Nothing in his school records. No incidents at all."

"I said he *could* be our guy, Riley," she snapped. "Could be. You want to blame Hendricks for tunnel vision, but you're just as much to blame. The evidence—"

"Is painting quite the picture," Zac interrupted, silencing them both.

"Zac?" Morgan asked.

"Oh," he chirped. "Did you forget about little ol' me? The third wheel buzzing in your ear? Or were you too busy squabbling to—"

"Out with it, Zac."

The analyst sighed. "She said, not caring how cold and tired her colleague is from sitting in the cramped backseat of their car. I thought we paid top dollar for rentals? We couldn't afford something bigger? Imposing, even?"

Morgan cleared her throat. "Zac, she said, losing patience."

"I know how he's doing it." All paused on the line. Zac held his breath for a moment as his fingers clacked along the keyboard, the echo rising through the speaker. When he returned to the conversation, his smile was present in his voice. "I know the truth about Henry Reed."

CHAPTER TWENTY-ONE

What am I doing here?

Zac's excuses failed him on every level. A vacation to visit family? Where had he come up with such a lame story? He hadn't, and that was the problem. It was the cover offered for the assignment, one Zac had failed to refuse. That's what always happened when it came to making a decision. He never made one. Someone else did.

His parents were the same way, full of regret, filled to the brim with meaningless tasks and never able to look past them. They funneled those desires, those grand wishes into Zac and buried him with them. Their expectations were dressed up as his responsibilities. They decided everything from his choice of college to his major. From corporate work in the private sector to that wonderful dream of a government pension at retirement, there was no question on his part. All had been determined by others. He didn't mind—not when he found an aptitude for the work. He enjoyed the idea of service to his country and by default the responsibility set by his family.

He'd married the girl next door, the obvious choice. Claire gave him the gift of fatherhood and never wished anything on him but the best. Not that he knew what that meant. There was only family and work. Nothing sparked within Zac, no impulsive choices. There was only responsibility and expectations.

Coming to Chicago was a fine example. Field work was never something he wanted. He preferred his cubicle and his tasks. Easy, simplistic, and straightforward. The work he accomplished helped people. This task? This didn't help *anyone*, not even him.

Part of him thought that might change. For so long he'd listened to the same music, read the same books, ate the same meals every week. Nothing changed. Nothing deviated. Part of Zac thought field work might make the difference — that *he* could make a difference and in doing so wake up to a new world. It had not gone as planned.

"Zac?"

Morgan's voice echoed over his clicking fingers. He ignored her to focus on the search algorithm running through a number of viable options on his laptop. Each needed to be explored fully and he did so quickly and quietly, despite bringing the discovery to the attention of Ben and Morgan before he was prepared.

The tension between them threatened to pull the mission down around their heads. Years as Head of Operational Support and Research had shown him it was a dangerous combination in the field. His presence did nothing to assuage that tension. His questioned explanation only added to their mounting frustration.

He had seen teams develop. He had been there when Grissom first brought Morgan and Lincoln into the fold. They went through their own growing pains, a crucible each member faced at the hands of the DSA's work. Each made the best of the situation, each persevered — Morgan especially. After three years working together, Zac understood the woman better than most. Her kindness, her resolve, her care over the people affected by the work — all matched his own hopes when it came to what they were hoping to accomplish, what Zac dreamed the DSA was capable of achieving.

"Any time now, Zac," she repeated.

"Sorry," he muttered. He flipped through windows until landing on his top result. Sifting through data was difficult considering the amounts flooding the laptop, but a quick scan allowed him to clear the palate efficiently. "Yeah, I have him."

"Reed?"

"Yeah. Henry David Reed."

"How did you find him?"

They didn't actually want a technical explanation. They didn't want to know about the databases hacked or the illegal maneuvers he would no doubt have to list in his report after the fact. They needed a story, the story they had been searching for since finding out about the mysterious Mr. Reed.

"Well, a cursory look kept bringing up little more than we already know," he started, fingers to his earpiece to keep it in place. "Clean-cut kid living at home with his mom. No digital footprint to speak of, nothing to speak of their activities. No memberships to organizations. No charitable donations. Not even tax records in the system. Meaning, he had help keeping it that way."

"And the info?" Morgan pressed.

Zac sighed. The truth about analysis was that for the thousand pages of information discovered about an individual, when it came to what was useful—or what an agent in the field found useful—only one page ended up being necessary. He found his one page and let the info fill the screen.

"Ever hear of Edgewater Medical Center?" He paused, then shook his head. "I'll take the heavy breathing as a big fat no on that. Okay. Two decades ago a large portion of the hospital burned to the ground. A fast-moving fire took out an entire wing in seconds. The maternity ward, in fact."

"No," the former doctor whispered.

"Yeah," he continued, drawing it out. "Not a Hallmark movie of the week. Over one hundred casualties. When crews were able to clear the place they found two survivors buried under some debris. I'll give you two guesses who they were."

"Henry."

"And his mother," Morgan broke through the line. "Got it. Her records still in the system? Some sign of what could have changed them?"

"No. Not through HIPAA or protected health information. This was before any off-site servers kept backups. No cloud to help me out."

"I'm sensing a but in there of the *look-how-smart-I-am* variety," Ben said.

"Absolutely," Morgan agreed.

Zac grinned. "You know me so well. Hospital records were lost, but I did find her OBGYN. It was a defunct clinic that was home to barely a dozen patients over a five-year span."

"Did you find anything strange in her file?"

"Besides the fact that it was firewalled up the wazoo?" Zac asked, switching screens. His security measures flared and he struggled to maintain the connection while hoping for enough time to take what he needed. "I'm talking government-level protocols set in place that are sending red flags to who knows how many people. But yeah, it looks like she was given more than the typical prenatal vitamins. There was something else in her monthly regimen—something called Promethean."

"A drug trial?"

"Not on any public record," Zac replied. He pulled the file and dropped it into a secure hub before disconnecting. When the security alerts diminished, he let out a relaxed breath. "There are notes here on other clinics, including shipments received from a number of companies."

"The other fires," Ben said.

Zac confirmed the names and addresses offered by Hendricks. "Every single one. The only reason there is any information is someone forgot to scrub this server. They simply closed the office. Must have been forgotten."

"Now we have our connection between the fires, at least."

"Any details on the drug?"

He typed feverishly, falling behind the mounting questions. The extensive file provided information dated throughout the five-year lifespan of the clinic. Each patient was clearly listed, and he started a separate search for each of the other women under their care. Yet there was nothing about the drug itself—the sections redacted or missing entirely.

"Not a one," he said.

"Don't really need any," Ben said. "Not with the name."

"Prometheus. He stole fire from the gods," Morgan said.

"And gave it to man."

"What a gift."

"Yeah," Zac said. "And guess who was involved in producing the drug, albeit under different names, corporate structures, yadda, yadda, yadda..."

"Shur-Rite."

"And Reginald Kane."

"What about the other patients for the trial, Zac?" Ben asked.

"I'm running the names now, but it doesn't look good," he said. Death certificates were the results, ten names over the five-year period the clinic was open. "Anna Reed was the only one lucky enough to come out of the clinic, from what I can find."

"The only one to come to term, then."

"Henry could be looking for some revenge?" Morgan said.

"Something about that doesn't seem right to me."

"You think he's being played?"

"If so, he's not the only one," Ben grumbled. "Zac? See if anyone else on that list has a relative or loved one in the city. Maybe we aren't casting a wide-enough net."

"I'll keep digging."

"We're on our way," Ben said.

"Good, I'm—" The comm line died, the sound of his colleagues immediately gone from his ear. He removed the piece and dropped it on the backseat passenger-side cushion. They didn't need him any longer. The information ran through their heads and any connection made would come from them. Their backgrounds were ideal for putting puzzles together. He merely threw the pieces on the table.

Yet one piece stood out for him: Edgewater Medical Center. It was an abandoned facility just north of the city. Was there something more to be learned from the hospital? Something he had missed? He scribbled a note, though he dropped it at the sound of a knock on the back door of the rental.

Zac clutched his chest. "Dammit, Riley. Why the hell—?"

The figure outside grabbed at the handle. Zac, confused, struggled to focus as the shadow took form.

Henry Reed stood beside the car with his fist pulled back.

"Wait!"

Henry's hand shattered the glass of the car. Heat flooded the interior despite the cold of the winter night. Glass covered Zac. His trembling fingers struggled to shove the note into the seat cushion to hide it from view. Terror caused his entire body to shake. His fear was not due to the anger building in his attacker's face. It came from the hand of his attacker.

A hand engulfed in flame.

"I hear you've been looking for me."

CHAPTER TWENTY-TWO

A slow walk from the storage unit steadied a weary Ben Riley. Zac's information had been crucial. The drug trial finally shed much-needed light on the secret hidden behind Reginald Kane's death. It had failed to vindicate his feelings about their lead suspect, however, and that concerned him.

Revenge for what had been done to his mother might explain why Henry targeted Kane. When Ben took into account the boy's mother his theory fell apart. Motivation was critical and only fit half the situation instead of the whole puzzle.

Morgan mirrored his unspoken sentiments. She waited near the sidewalk, coffee cup tossed in the closest receptacle. No greeting was exchanged. From her perspective, none was warranted.

Both stopped at the corner. The back window on the driver's side of their rental car lay in pieces scattered on the street. More glass was scattered within the vehicle, reflecting the streetlights.

"Zac..."

Morgan rushed to the car, gun in hand yet tucked close. She skirted through the traffic and scanned the wreckage before reaching the sidewalk on the passenger side.

"Is he—?" Ben joined her on the opposite side, mindful of the traffic honking at his presence in the street. The glass extended beyond the car. It scattered across the lane. "They're going to cancel the DSA's rental agreement for sure."

Morgan's glare cut through him worse than any condemnation.

"Sorry."

"You damn well should be," she snapped. Her hand ran

along her brow. Pain filled her eyes when she grazed the bandage along her forehead.

"I said I was."

"What the hell was I thinking?" she said, pacing along the vehicle. "Why the hell were we even here?"

"We were doing the job, Morgan," Ben replied. She didn't care to hear it, and continued ignoring him. "What do we have?"

She stopped in mid-stride. "Besides a missing member of my team?"

"We'll find him." Morgan's head shook vehemently. She was too busy denouncing their actions; every poor decision was put at his feet, but the burden of those choices lay with her. Ben tried to break through her silent rumination. "We will, Morgan. We will."

She let out a calming breath. "Right."

"Morgan…"

"I said all right, Riley."

"Okay," he responded. He backed off from the car, glass crunching beneath his feet. "So what do we have?"

The back door opened and she sifted through the debris. Careful to avoid the glass, she tucked her hand inside her sleeve, then brushed off the cloth interior as she searched. "Not much."

Ben nodded. They were finally making progress with the case. What little headway they had made came at a cost. The frustrated agent sighed, and he let his head fall to his chest. Catching the light perfectly along the side panel, Ben stopped. His eyes went wide at the slight indent along the car door beneath the shattered window.

"Maybe more than you think." He tracked the indent up and down the ridges forged into the steel. "Henry."

"What?" She left the confines of the car to join him. Ben stood to give her access to the dent etched into the side panel. It was burned and seared for all to see.

A hand.

"Hard to mistake that signature."

"Why would he — ?"

"Hey," Ben said. He reached for her shoulder, but she shuffled away, unwilling to accept the comfort. "Morgan, we don't know what happened yet. Let's stick with what we do know."

Morgan opened the back door and sat down along the punctured cloth. She closed her eyes, body poised as if reliving Zac's final moments in the vehicle after their communication silenced.

Returning to her search, Morgan found a notepad resting on the seat. "Looks like he was able to leave some notes. Not many though."

"No laptop or tablet?" Ben leaned along the broken window, careful to avoid the shards stuck in the frame.

"Is that strange?"

"We're talking about a kid that can control fire. So I suppose it isn't. Just don't see the point in taking them."

"Wait a second."

Ben leaned close. Morgan pulled a single slip of paper, torn along the corner, from between the seats. "What is it?"

She smiled, a rare treat during their stay in Chicago. "Zac, you smart son of a bitch."

"Not what I would personally call him, but all right."

"He had it. It was right in front of him, but he didn't get the chance to tell us." Ben backed up, allowing Morgan to exit the car. She passed along the note.

EDGEWATER MEDICAL CENTER.

"The hospital he was talking about?" Ben asked, confused. "Where Reed was born?"

"The *abandoned* hospital, yes."

"Wait. You think he's there?"

Her head tilted, clearly weighing her thoughts. "We know where Henry lives. His mother's dead. He's scared but smart. The smart will keep him out of sight."

Ben nodded as he followed her train of thought. "But the fear will take him somewhere familiar."

"Comfortable. Safe."

"And private," Ben finished, a wry smirk on his lips. "I'll drive."

Morgan shook her head, cutting him off. "Just get in the car, Riley."

CHAPTER TWENTY-THREE

Spit dotted the sidewalk, a long trail of saliva running into a thick crack. Connor Hendricks kicked his foot off the wall of the building and followed the strand. His gait, slow and sure, allowed him time to process the scene down the street.

The two DSA agents jumped inside their beat-up rental and shot into traffic like a bullet. Horns blared and curse words rose—the only personal interaction available on the road these days. Not that anyone raced much farther than the next street light, where the angry words and gestures were allowed to percolate between commuters.

Hendricks relaxed, allowing the car to reach the end of the next block before moving for his waiting ride. He would have been more at ease over the situation had he arrived five minutes earlier. Shattered glass crunched under traffic, the actions of Henry Reed clear from across the street.

Five minutes made all the difference. Three hundred extra seconds stuck in traffic after receiving Morgan's message on his phone. Five lousy minutes and Hendricks could have ended the entire affair quietly, without the need for further violence.

Now violence was the only option left to him.

Riley and Dunleavy knew where they were headed. During his absence they had learned more about the young man—the truth he had attempted to keep hidden. Promethean. Henry was the last remaining element of the decades-old project. It was time to bring him home. One way or another, it was time to end this.

If only Hendricks had those five minutes back.

He spit again. It hit his car and wiped the salt coating the side in a thin stream. He circled the vehicle, finger on the remote. The doors unlocked, the trunk released, and he caught the hinge during the upswing. He kept it low, peering inside the darkened space. The light had been removed to keep the cargo private.

He had covered the body with a thin tarp. Terror rested in the dead man's cold stare. His hands were frozen from rigor mortis, spread wide in front of his chest. Hendricks removed the FBI jacket and tossed it at the corpse. The shoulders were too tight, the sleeves too cramped.

In its place he reached for a black vest and strapped the thick fabric over his chest. A bag slipped into his waiting hand and he paused to give one last satisfied glare at the dead man in the trunk. He had served his purpose.

The trunk slammed shut. From the side of the duffel Hendricks took out a radio, bringing it to life with the click of a switch on the side.

"Are you in position?"

Static rang through the small speaker. Hendricks slipped inside the driver's seat and settled against the cloth backing. The bag fell along the passenger side, the glint of a pistol reflecting the moonlight filtering from above.

"Trailing them now," the radio chirped. The voice was steady and calculating, the way Hendricks preferred to work. It was something he'd missed during his time in Chicago, working with outsiders in an effort to close the loop of information pertaining to Kane's death. The entire operation had been a mistake from top to bottom. His handler would hear about it when this was finished.

"Have you been spotted?" Hendricks asked, though he already knew the answer. He didn't work with amateurs. He demanded the best from all under his employ. Simple verification was all he required with the question, especially considering the faults of the last week. Nothing could go wrong from this point forward.

"Negative. They appear… preoccupied," the man on the other end said, holding out the final word as if considering an alternative.

Preoccupied was the correct word choice when it came to the DSA agents. Hendricks had noticed it with each interaction of the DSA agents. They were raw, inexperienced, at least when it came to working together. They had no bond, no commitment to the other.

It had cost them their colleague. It would cost them much more by the end of the night.

The engine turned over, exhaust kicking out with the rising heat blowing from the vents. Hendricks eased into traffic, comfortable and relaxed as he followed the growing caravan moving north out of the city.

"Stick close," he said to the SUV in clear view two blocks ahead. "It's time to end this."

CHAPTER TWENTY-FOUR

Zac stirred, and his head pulsed with pain. His eyes struggled to focus. The haze of the room ranged from blurry to imperceptible. His right arm shot up to assist in clearing his vision only to be pulled back to his side, a clatter ringing from the radiator along the wall behind him.

"What?" he muttered at the handcuffs locked around his wrist. Suddenly, the world sharpened. The room was dismal looking. A single bulb in the center provided a cone of light barely able to pierce the shadows along the periphery. Stray carts rested along the right-hand wall. Dusty old machines lay scattered on the ground—heart rate monitors, blood pressure sleeves, oxygen tanks, and the like. A stack of metal chairs leaned precariously against the left-hand wall. A storage room or overflow of some kind, his location clear from the markings hanging outside the door.

Edgewater Medical Center.

"Oh, no," Zac whispered, free hand over his lips. He recalled the hand reaching for him in the car. Henry's burning hand. It had grabbed his leg, searing heat ran up his body for an instant, and then darkness.

He must have blacked out. *So much for acting like a field agent.* Where were Ben and Morgan? Had they realized he was missing? How much time had he lost?

Zac pulled at the cuff, the metal digging into his wrist. "Come on, come on."

"Sorry about that."

Zac cried out, the shadow in the door approaching slowly. Henry carried Zac's laptop under his arm. He dropped it into a nearby chair and wheeled it over toward the worried tech.

"Precaution."

"From me?" Zac asked, his voice cracking.

The young man shrugged. "You never know."

"I suppose so."

Henry pointed to the computer and smiled. "The processor in here is amazing. Quad core?"

Zac hesitated as the chair came to rest beside him. He pulled the laptop loose and cradled it like a lost child. "Next-gen model. And thanks?"

"You're welcome," Henry said with a nod. His hand reached for the captured analyst.

"Hey! Don't—!" Zac cried. He waited for the end, struggling to keep his eyes open and not fade to black once more. He wanted to face what was coming, thoughts of Claire and their son bubbling to the surface. He thought of everything left unsaid and the dreams he had lost due to the choices made by others.

His cuff fell away from his wrist. It rang along the radiator. "Why?" he uttered. "Why would you—?"

Henry stepped away. After grabbing a chair from the stack, he joined Zac. "You've been out for a bit and I wasn't sure what I was going to do when you woke. I haven't been sure of anything in a few days. But I've been going through your notes. You didn't kill my mom."

"What?" Zac exclaimed. He struggled to the chair, the back nearly toppling over at his presence. "Of course we didn't—"

"Like I said," Henry continued, "I know that now. You're free to go if you want or..."

He trailed off, then jumped to his feet. Quick steps back into the hall left the wary analyst unsure of the direction of their conversation. With the pause, Zac opened the laptop. The screen came to life without issue. He ran a quick scan to ensure his protocols were intact, though he was surprised Henry would have been able to find anything of use with his security measures.

Henry returned with two paper bags, grease collecting at the base of each. Zac's brow furrowed. "What is this?"

"Fast-food-pick-me-up." Henry opened the bag, the smell of French fries filling the air. Zac's stomach churned with hunger. "Cold but it's still delicious. Promise."

Zac hesitated until the bag was handed over by his captor.

There was no denying his hunger. Food had been an afterthought all day, his time with Ben and Morgan wrapped up in their search. One look at the Chicago-style hot dog with its yellow mustard coating, white onions, and sweet pickle relish was all that was needed to sway him. The addition of a slice of tomato and celery salt made it a hodgepodge of toppings on the steamed all-beef frankfurter. The overwhelmed tech summed up the experience with one word:

Heaven.

They ate in silence, devouring every last scrap. Henry put Zac to shame despite his lean, muscular frame compared to Zac's less-than-prime physical condition. He pounded down two dogs and a bag of fries in a matter of minutes.

In the aftermath, both rested against their chairs with sated appetites. Zac, lost in thought, broke out in a smile. He leaned forward to place his leftovers at his side. "I have to say… Weirdest abduction of all time?"

Henry laughed. "I strive to be unique."

"Speaking of…"

"Yeah," Henry said. He stood and paced the length of the floor. Zac waited patiently, not wanting to push. Henry let out a sigh. "So you know the truth."

"We do."

He rubbed his neck and took a long breath. Extending his left hand out, he snapped two fingers and a small flame burst to life from his thumb. It danced along his skin, traveling around each finger until resting against his palm.

"Can you imagine having to be in complete control every moment of your life?"

Zac couldn't. He had never controlled anything in his life. Every choice was an expectation, one bought and paid for by others looking out for his best interests. Not that he even knew what those were anymore.

"I'd say yes, but you definitely take it to a whole new level."

Henry smirked. "Let's just say temper tantrums at home ended with torched curtains on more than one occasion. But I'm a quick study."

"I could tell," Zac said. Henry's eyebrow rose. "The books at the storage unit."

"Right," Henry replied. "When I was young. I found I could

burn hot for a short time, but then I needed a long recharge peri-od. It was mostly from the fear of what was happening to me. Not like there was a counseling group for it, but my mom did her best with what little she knew. I figured the more I under-stood about my body the more safe I would be. Saying that out loud sounds like a horrible PSA for a Sex Ed Class."

"I wasn't going to make the joke." They shared the laugh like old friends. The flame died along Henry's hand, and he sat back down across from Zac. "Henry, why were you there that night at Shur-Rite?"

The young man sighed. "My mom was supposed to be. I guess she's been doing it for some time. I could say it was to pro-tect me, but I'll never know now, will I?" He took a breath, the memory of his mother resting in sad eyes. "Anyway, she's been sick. Real sick. I thought I could help her out. Take care of her like she did for me for so long. When he pulled that gun on me I thought it was over. I thought I'd never get a chance to do any-thing with my life—not even get a chance to say goodbye to her."

"And you lost control."

Hands clasped tight to his knees. "I killed a man. He tried to hurt me. Tried to do more than hurt me, but that's not a justifica-tion."

"It wasn't your fault."

Henry shook his head. He was back on his feet to pace the vacant room. "I never should have gone."

"Who sent you?" Zac asked. "Who has your mother been working for?"

"Some guy called me this morning," Henry said, working it out as he spoke. "He said she had been an asset for his group. His voice was like fire and brimstone. I'd heard it before, but it took me a while to figure out from where."

"Henry?"

"You have too," the young man resumed. "You were with him last night at Jen-Pad."

"At Jen-Pad?" Zac's eyes widened. "Oh, hell."

Hendricks.

CHAPTER TWENTY-FIVE

Morgan pulled the car into the parking lot of Edgewater Medical Center. She quietly cursed every minute of the journey north of the city. Every red light. Every pedestrian crossing. Every breath Ben took in the passenger seat beside her. Zac was missing, and she refused to let another member of the team fall.

Her team. That made them her responsibility.

Her chest tightened at the thought. She couldn't handle another loss, another person she had failed to truly connect with on any real level. All centered on a geeky tech she had nothing in common with except their place of employment.

The sedan was cold—freezing from the broken window that allowed the wind to cut through the cabin. The temperature didn't affect her. She felt white hot under her coat.

By the rear of the lot, outside the burned and abandoned section of the medical center, Morgan found another vehicle: the light blue truck that was missing from Anna Reed's driveway when they visited. Rust crawled along the doors and up from the undercarriage. It was an easily recognizable mode of transportation, yet it had somehow eluded an all-points bulletin posted by the FBI. She spun the wheel hard, bringing the car aside the truck, then slammed the rental into park.

She clenched her jaw as she caught sight of Ben's concerned-puppy-dog look. She refused to meet his gaze, to engage with him any further. Instead, she released the Glock from its holster at her hip. She checked the clip, knowing it remained full, and then opened her door. A hand clasped her shoulder, stopping her.

"Whoa there, Morgan."

"Riley," Morgan said through gritted teeth. "The hand. Now."

Ben pulled away. "I get it."

"Then what is your problem?"

"What do you plan on doing?"

"Are you kidding?" she asked. She tightened her grip on her sidearm.

Ben sat back. "I don't think I am. I mean, I might be but… No. Not this time."

Morgan stepped out of the vehicle. "Come on."

Ben followed suit. By the time he was free of his seatbelt and out of the rental Morgan was halfway to the main entrance of the former hospital.

"Morgan," he called, trying to stop her. She hustled for the entrance. "Henry—"

"Assaulted our colleague and has him in there doing God knows what."

Ben slammed his hand on the hood of the car. "Hopefully not talking to him, cause what's the point, right?"

"You smug son of a bitch."

"There it is," Ben announced, arms outstretched. His blood-stained tie whipped in the wind.

"What?"

"I've been waiting. This whole time, in fact. You've played the distant bitch real well, Morgan. Refused to even *try* to make this work. You've been holding everything in. But now? Here comes the volcano."

Ben circled her, stopping with the entrance at his back. Morgan tapped her gun along the grip. "Get out of my way."

"No."

The weapon leveled on his chest. "Dammit, Riley."

"I said no," Ben replied, his arms crossed. "You want to take a shot at me? Fine. You've been doing it the entire time anyway. May as well make it official."

She sucked in each breath hard, filling her lungs to the brim before exhaling. "Like you should talk. You're incapable of having a real conversation with a person."

"That is true. But at least I admit it. And I still talk."

"About what?" Morgan screamed. Every second they wasted was another Zac wasn't with them. Yet she couldn't find the words. Couldn't find a way to convey it to a man she had only known a smattering of weeks. Her anger was all she knew when she looked into his dusty eyes. "What the hell do you want me to talk to you about?"

"Anything," Ben said. "Come on, Morgan. What did I *do*? What have any of us done to you? Really?"

"Nothing," she snapped. "Not a damn thing."

"I need you to trust me, Morgan."

"Trust you? How can I?" The gun stayed on his chest. Her finger inched toward the trigger without thought. "Even now you're pushing Henry Reed as the victim when he has Zac!"

Ben backed off, hands in the air. "I'm not pushing anything. I have doubts for sure, but they don't influence the choices I make. Same with anything I'm feeling at the moment."

"It's that kind of crap—"

"Say it." Ben stepped toward her and she backed away to maintain the space between them. "Just say it already."

"You're insufferable. You make decisions without thinking. Decisions that impact the rest of us. That impact my team."

"Don't make this about me, Morgan. Don't lie to yourself right now," Ben pressed.

"He is my responsibility. Same as you. I have to—"

"I don't believe you," Ben replied with the shake of his head. She cringed as he hit every button, every layer of frustration collected within her for so long. Every swallowed bit of regret and guilt.

"Fine. You want to know why I didn't want you here in the first place? You want to know why I don't trust you? Why I *can't* trust you?"

"More than anything."

"You're going to get me killed! Just like…" Her words came out so fast, like a thought buried for too long. It was a reaction that resulted from every interaction, every conversation with the newly-minted field agent at the DSA.

Ben fell on his heels, the breath sucked out of him. "Like Ruth? Morgan, I…"

As stunned as he was by the confession, it was Morgan who took the brunt of her admission. The gun fell to her side, her other hand clutched tight to her bruised brow with eyes awake for the first time since his arrival. "Oh, God. No. I know, Riley. I know that it wasn't you. That you didn't... Why did I say that?"

"Because you've wanted to ever since I showed up for this case."

She felt the breeze on her cheeks, surprised it was accompanied by soft tears running from her eyes. She rubbed them away. "Yeah," she admitted. "I think I did."

Ben smirked. "I'm not asking you to trust me implicitly, Morgan. I'm just asking for an inch."

"Yet you trust me."

"My old man always told me to never anger a woman taller than me."

"Smart man."

"I do trust you, Morgan. You're driven and compassionate. You know the right play here. With Henry."

"Do I?"

"You do." Ben started for the door. A padlock lay broken and discarded in the snow nearby. The metal scraped along the frame but pulled free, opening to darkness within. "Let's go get our guy."

She stood and let the cold rush through her. It chilled her for the first time all evening. It was freeing, a great weight released. There had been so many mistakes in her life. Her time in the Army had shrouded every decision she had made since. Yet here was a man taking a chance on her. Ben relied on her judgment and more.

Her friendship.

"Morgan?"

"He's nine."

"Who?" Ben asked, confused.

"My nephew." She moved for the door. Ben released the clip on his Ruger, keeping it low and tight to his right side. Her Glock slid against her palm, steady and controlled. "You asked about him before. He's nine."

CHAPTER TWENTY-SIX

They worked systematically. Their steps carried them from the first-floor entrance to the rehabilitation wing. Flashlights guided them from door to door, each moving fluidly in tune with the other.

It was like waking up from a nightmare. For the first time since Ben's arrival he was part of the team, working *with* Morgan instead of around her—no longer afraid of the reaction to a joke or snide comment. She was different as well. The burden of leading faded behind the search, and she was refocused on the task at hand.

Zac was alive. They knew that going into the hospital. Now, after days of hunting through the city, it was only a matter of finding him so they could get answers.

The rehab ward led to a series of branched corridors. Signage indicated the ICU to the right and a blocked-off emergency ward to the left. Straight ahead were the stairs to the second floor and the maternity ward, the very same that had burned with the birth of Henry Reed.

Ben took the lead. Instinct allowed them to remain silent in their search. Morgan's reversal filled him with a confidence he had not known since starting his tenure at the DSA. Morgan had offered her hand in trust, and he had taken it.

He couldn't help but wonder how far it extended. How much to convey to her, to share about his growing concerns. Should he tell her about the house on Wex and the secrets locked within? Or mention his current predicament with the men in the sedans, those tracking his every movement and listening to his every word in his apartment?

Or was Morgan involved to a degree? Was she testing him?

More doubts, though he refused to surrender to them in the midst of their hunt.

A nurse's station met them at the heart of the ward. Oxygen tanks sat in piles along the inner wall. Broken blinds flapped against shattered and cracked window frames. Lights flickered, and it seemed power had been intentionally diverted to the wing. They lowered their flashlights, then tucked them away. Their weapons stayed out though—they used them to edge along each door for a sign of life.

The sound of a clacking keyboard clued them in to the presence within a room prior to the nurse's station. Morgan turned the corner, sidearm poised, then she lowered it quickly.

"Zac."

Ben smiled as she rushed inside. Zac peered up from his laptop at her approach and waved.

"Hey, guys."

She crouched beside him, pulling his head close. "Damn you, Zac."

"What took you so long?" he asked.

She batted him away playfully. "When are you going to learn to keep that mouth shut?" He shrugged and she helped him to his feet. "You all right?"

"Oh, I'm allowed to talk now?" he asked with a grin. "I'm fine. So is Henry."

"Where is he?" Ben stayed near the door. He peered around the corridor for signs of the firebrand.

"Don't worry about that yet." Zac waved him closer. "He's innocent though. Just like you thought."

"You'll make me blush, Mr. Modine," Ben said.

"His mother was being used as an asset. He's not sure for what agency."

"He give any specifics?" Morgan inquired.

"Enough to identify one of the players involved," Zac said, eyes locked on Ben. It took a split second for Ben to recognize the answer behind the glare.

"Aw, come on," Ben groaned. "Don't say it."

"Connor Hendricks," a voice announced from the hall. All turned toward the new arrival. Henry Reed spread his hands open for them to see. No flames. No threatening measures. He was just a kid, weary from the fight. "Or so Zac here tells me, anyway."

"Henry."

"I'm sorry about your car."

Ben shrugged. "We bought the melted-handprint, broken-window insurance package. Don't worry about it. As long as Zac here—"

"I'm fine." Zac pawed through the paper bag by his feet and jammed a couple French fries into his mouth.

"We can see that." Morgan shook her head.

"Anyone want to talk about our friend Hendricks?" Ben asked.

"He killed my mom, didn't he?"

To Ben, there was no question. Adding Hendricks to the mix finally brought the whole puzzle into focus, snapping the final piece into place. "Yeah, Henry. We're pretty sure he did."

The kid leaned against the wall. "If only I hadn't opened that stupid package. My mom, she's been so sick and… I didn't mean to kill that man at Shur-Rite."

"We know."

Henry swiped at tears in his eyes. "This isn't the first time she received one of these packages. It's been going on for years. Could my mom really have—?"

Ben stopped him, hand on the kid's shoulder. "She was used, same as you have been."

"So what now?"

"Zac?"

He turned to Morgan. "We have to get him out of here."

"We will," Ben said, calm against the analyst's concerns.

Morgan stepped between them. "It isn't that simple. He killed a man."

"In self-defense!" Zac exclaimed.

Her brown eyes thinned. "You've seen what he can do. How do we walk out of here like nothing has happened?"

"Hendricks will—"

"Do nothing," Ben finished.

"He's FBI, Riley."

"There's a reason he's kept us at arm's length. Why he's tried to cut us out of the search for Henry since the beginning. He's been so adamant to pursue Henry right from the start."

"That isn't—"

"How tall was Anna Reed's killer?"

Morgan paused, following his train of thought. "Six foot."

"Same as Hendricks," Ben continued. "Who found the murder weapon?"

"Hendricks, but—"

"The slugs matched the one fired at Shur-Rite. It was Reginald Kane's gun," Ben confirmed. "Were any prints found on the gun?"

"None. It was wiped down."

"Does that sound right to you?" Ben asked. "Any of it? Or was it merely convenience, a story Hendricks put together for us to swallow?"

"Ben..."

"Let's say I'm right. We get Henry out of here. If we turn him over to the FBI, here and now, we will lose control of the situation." She started to argue, but he held her back with a finger. "If I'm wrong, he's still in our custody and we bring him in."

"Morgan," Zac pleaded. "The DSA might have resources available to help Henry. Metcalf could figure out what to do with him."

"This has been fun," Henry said, causing all parties to remember his presence. "Standing here while you determine my guilt or innocence and decide my fate. I'm right here, you know?"

"Good," Morgan said. "Then we won't have to repeat everything later."

"Depends on where you landed on what to do."

"Let's get moving," she said as she let out a long breath.

Henry cracked a smile. "Then I'm good."

"Excellent." Ben started for the door. "Let's—"

The lights flickered and faded before dropping the floor into darkness. Emergency reds ran along the hall, the backup generator still functioning thanks to its recent inhabitant.

"Crap," Henry muttered.

"Yeah," Zac called. He pulled at the torn curtain covering the window and stared at the parking lot below. "Remember that part about us swallowing Hendricks' story and doing his work for him?"

"Unfortunately." Ben joined the tech at the window. Two additional vehicles sat in the parking lot. There was no movement outside, which meant only one thing. They were already in the building.

"Looks like we closed the case for him."

Morgan started for the door, pulling Henry behind her. All four entered the hall in a rush for the exit. They skidded to a halt instantly at the presence blocking their one and only exit. "We also closed us in here with—"

Hendricks stood with three others, all dressed in head-to-toe black body armor. Hendricks carried a pistol, while automatic rifles rested in the hands of his team. Night-vision goggles gave them a clear view of their targets. Even in the darkness Ben noted the sneer on the face of Hendricks. He leveled his weapon on them and his wetwork team joined his movement.

"And you have my thanks for your efforts."

CHAPTER TWENTY-SEVEN

"This is Morgan. Leave a short one, wouldja?"

The message tone chimed and Lincoln hung up for the third time in the past hour. He sat along the frigid concrete steps of the Central Library, unsure why he continued to hesitate. The call took on a sudden importance now that he held a clear direction on the Witness' whereabouts—though, for the life of him, Lincoln failed to understand why.

Nor did he understand why her lack of an answer bothered him, and why her voice might calm the storm building inside him as he held the note left by the man who had taken Ruth from the world.

DES MOINES

THREE DAYS

YOU KNOW WHERE

Lincoln crumpled the message into his pocket and vacated the steps of the library. His Jeep chirped at his approach, the doors unlocked and ready to accept his anxious frame. He stopped at the trunk first. He rummaged through his duffel bag to make sure his supplies had remained intact. An ample amount of gear stared back at him. From a flak jacket to a high-powered rifle, he was prepared for what came next.

So was the Witness.

Lincoln rubbed his eyes. No matter how he looked at the information left out like bread crumbs, there was no getting around the fact that the Witness played the long game against them—and the man was winning. It exhausted the soldier and he slammed the trunk shut without another glance.

Stephanie waited for his report. Messages chimed on the hour, every hour, for an update on his situation. There were calls every other, the last one frantic for some word as to his progress. She had Metcalf to worry about. Out in the field, there was no one but him and the job at hand.

Des Moines.

Four years later, the incident still trailed him like a damn shadow. It had grown into an all-consuming entity intent on swallowing every light in his life. Four years, yet the memory burned his eyes. He rested against the side of the Jeep, the cool air swirling around him.

The phone sat in his hand. One call would bring Metcalf into the loop and put a common-sense plan into action. Metcalf at tactical and the field team as backup, everyone following the same path to the room where their target waited, each willing to pull the trigger when the time came.

Instead, it had to be him. For Ruth. For Bellbrook. No one else understood what had been taken from them by this man. For Lincoln, it was a chance at a life never sought, one never thought deserved. Ruth faded to memory, but the concept of her, the idealized version of some far-distant future never to be discovered, remained for Lincoln. He fought for that ideal just as much as he fought for his country. Who she was to him slipped into the ether, the great unknown quagmire of the past, but who she *could have been* remained with him.

The Witness had taken that from Lincoln and would pay for it with his life. One more target. One more death. And then he would be free of the pain running through his body.

"This is Morgan. Leave a short one, wouldja?"

The phone clicked, and he lowered it to his side in frustration once more. Morgan needed to hear it from him — the justification of what was to come. Not through a message, but from him directly. They had been recruited at practically the same time, trained together. The pain of war had followed them as easily as their mistakes. She would understand the necessity of his actions.

Or did he call for another reason? For her to talk him out of it? Her ideals always favored life. His went in a different direction. Maybe they weren't as similar as he hoped.

He thumbed the screen of the phone and pulled up the extension saved under the letter S. Stephanie picked up after the first ring, her voice low and anxious.

"Lincoln? What did you find? Are you—?"

"I know where he is," Lincoln said, his voice as cold as the night. "I know what I have to do."

"I can support you on this," Stephanie answered. "Lincoln, let me help."

He took a long breath and closed his eyes. Whoever he was meant to be waited in Des Moines. It was time to find out what kind of man Lincoln MacKenzie was—alone.

"I'll be in touch when it's done."

The phone fell, skittering along the parking lot of the library. His boot finished the job. Pieces of the device scattered under his heel, though the crunching sound was lost to the grinding of his teeth.

He settled in the seat of the Jeep, his connection with the DSA severed. There was only him, the open road, and one last destination on the map.

Des Moines.

No matter the cost. For Ruth, for Bellbrook, and with every passing moment for himself. It was time to face the past and accept the future.

CHAPTER TWENTY-EIGHT

Gunshots erupted in all directions. Bullets forced Ben to take cover with the rest of his colleagues behind the nurse's station in the center of the abandoned maternity ward. Hendricks approached from the far end of the hall, not bothering to hide from the cacophony of violence. His compatriots split from the pack, two rushing along the right branch of the hall with the third taking the left.

Morgan kept the pair at bay. She timed her shots against those from the wetwork team. Her phone chimed, the chorus of *Baby Got Back* echoing several times before falling silent. It was the third time in as many minutes, and drew a look from her partner.

"You're pretty popular tonight," Ben shouted. He unloaded a pair of precision shots at the professional murderer moving to their left.

Her own shots rang out. A man's scream echoed as he fell; his hand clutched his knee. She smiled. "Must be that business line of credit I never applied for."

"I hear interest rates have never been better."

Zac shook his head. "Are you two really doing this right now?"

Ben jumped up and fired four shots, keeping the man to the left from circling around them. If one managed to round the branched hallways to their rear flank there would be no walking away.

"Don't think there are too many opportunities left, Zac." Ben dropped as a bevy of bullets soared overhead.

Morgan joined him. Her clip clattered against the ground.

"How bad?"

Ben jiggled his jacket pocket. "Two left."

"I'll go with very bad, then." She slammed a fresh clip in place, bullet ready in the chamber.

Hendricks was well-rested and had come prepared. Four men, all trained killers, and all wore body armor. Their weapons were M27 Infantry Automatic Rifles, a favorite of the United States Marine Corps. Why they wanted Henry was clear; too many eyes rested on the situation in Chicago, and he now stood as collateral.

They all did.

"We don't have to do it this way," Hendricks boomed, joy in his gravelly voice. "We only want the boy."

Morgan grumbled under her breath, and Ben laughed. "Don't worry, Morgan. I'm sure you made an impression on him too."

"Damn right I did." She spun, taking her shot. Hendricks didn't blink, didn't flinch from it, and allowed the bullet to strike center mass. It slammed into his vest, not even causing him to break his stride as he approached their position.

"Not nice, Agent Dunleavy," Hendricks said. "And it will cost you."

The still-standing member of the wetwork team on the right side took advantage of her anger and opened fire. Ben pulled her down, though a shot scraped along her shoulder while the rest clipped the wall on the other side of the hall. She cried out, the damage minimal but the pain clear.

Ben opened fire once again. Plaster ripped from the corner. The assault drove the man back, cutting him and his partner off from circling around their position. Ben took cover as the killer on his left flank took aim.

"You all right?"

"I will be," Morgan seethed.

"What do we do?" Zac asked, fear in his voice.

"I'm open to suggestions, Zac," Ben said. Morgan returned to her position and he did the same. He dislodged his clip, a replacement locked and loaded in the next breath. "Right about now would be great."

Zac opened his laptop, flinching with each bullet fired.

"I'll give you a pass, Riley!" Hendricks shouted. "A gift for leading me to him. You can go back to your DSA Batcave or whatever hole you work in, fill out your reports that everything is buttoned up, and forget the whole thing."

"Yeah," Ben yelled over the stray gunfire. "I'm not feeling very trusting, Hendricks. Since when does the FBI get in bed with illicit drug trials and murder?"

"FBI?" Hendricks guffawed. His laughter silenced his colleagues' assault. "Oh, Riley. I needed that. Thank you."

"You're welcome."

"You don't even see what's happening around you."

"Then explain it to me," Ben said, eyes locked on his target. Morgan maintained position on her own, unwilling to lose what little ground they had left.

"You're caught in the middle of something bigger than you can imagine," Hendricks said. "You think Bellbrook was the start of it? The people involved have been planning for a long time. You're not ready for what's coming, Riley. Make the smart play here."

Morgan opened fire, emptying the chamber before taking cover. "Good advice."

Ben followed suit. He drove the two men back one last time before draining his clip. "I'll be sure to remember it. Zac?"

"I need a minute."

"Time's up." Morgan grazed the tech's chin to pull his attention from the screen. "They're almost on top of us. Give us the best you've got."

Zac took a breath, cheeks flushed. "There's... There's a wing below us. The emergency ward."

"And a way out?" Ben had failed to notice one upon arriving.

"I... I think so."

"There is," Henry said.

"Yeah?"

Henry confirmed, "Yes."

Morgan peered over the counter. "How do we get there?"

"No idea."

Morgan slapped Ben's shoulder. He jammed his last clip into place. Staying low, he took aim and fired at the man on the right. The figure leapt back, then waited for the clicking of Ben's empty sidearm before racing across the gap.

"Shit," Ben announced. He dropped to the ground as the man on the left opened fire.

"That's it, then." Morgan closed her eyes.

"Maybe," Ben answered slowly.

"What are you thinking, Riley?"

Ben sighed. "You're not going to like it."

"What else is new?"

Ben ignored the comment, instead sliding close to Henry. The young man read the desperate look on his face. "Think you have it in you?"

"I have a choice?" Henry said.

"What?" Zac chimed in, confused. "Wait. Of course you do. Ben, tell him he has a choice."

"Zac," Morgan said, shaking her head.

"Henry?"

The young man nodded and rolled up his sleeves. "I need some space."

"Wait," Zac said. "What about after? Then what?"

"He knows," Ben said, his voice quiet and reserved. "Don't you?"

Henry Reed's hands burst into flame and he reached to the ground. "Yeah," he whispered. "I know what I have to do."

CHAPTER TWENTY-NINE

Connor Hendricks' patience had run out long ago. The call to bring him in had started the clock, the need for a cleanup of the Chicago situation bordering on routine. The DSA's involvement had brought nothing but roadblocks and sarcasm that grated every professional bone in the man's body.

It was time to put an end to it all.

"Come on, Riley," Hendricks called. His team had pinned the agents down behind a nurse's station in the center of the wing. Hendricks stayed patient, waiting for the kill shot. "We can talk about this. Just me and—"

A young man crawled out of the barrier. He rolled along the counter and landed on his feet just in front of the trigger-ready Hendricks.

"You," the agent said with a sneer. Henry Reed: the kid firebrand that had screwed up a simple operation. Reginald Kane's death had been supposed to come from Anna, a tried and true asset to the cause whether she wanted to be or not. Instead, Kane had burned and the public had found out. Now Henry was here, standing, ready for the end. "What do you think you're doing?"

"I give up," Henry announced, hands wide. "I'm coming in. I surrender. Whatever you want to call it."

"Just like that?"

"Looks like it," Henry said. "Now let the others go."

Hendricks peered through the young man with the sudden spine and smiled at his compatriot to the rear. A member of his wetwork team inched closer to the shrouded station and the rest of Henry's saviors. The other two maintained their positions on the branched corridors to provide cover. "Henry, they killed your—"

"No," Henry snapped. "No lies."

When Hendricks arrived he knew nothing about the kid. Henry's abilities had somehow slipped through the cracks of the Trust's tracking, a lost detail kept well-hidden by his mother. It was an incredible feat, especially considering their reach in every aspect of life. He blamed the ignorance on the complacency of certain members.

Henry was a special case. It wasn't the only one Hendricks had run into over the years. Some had been taken alive, studied for their talents. The experiments conducted had provided insight into the growing fluctuations of the human genome. Others, unfortunately, he was forced to put down.

Ever since Modine offered up Henry's name as their suspect, Hendricks had prepared for this moment. He'd hoped to turn the DSA against Henry, to force a confrontation between the two impediments to his success. The agents had proven irritatingly incapable of following the trail he left them. From the murder of Anna Reed to the other mysterious fires—those necessary to maintain the secrecy of the Trust's work—his prodding had done more to push Ben and his cohorts away than gain them as prospective allies. It had been his mistake and one he would not make again.

Since departing from them, Hendricks had turned his attention to Henry by studying his mother's thorough file and the testing completed by multiple agencies of her significant abilities. He knew what to expect. Her strengths, her limitations. All were shared by her son.

Still, the boy's confidence surprised him.

"I'm here, that's enough," Henry said. He wheeled around, a spectacle for the entire team. "But don't lie to me about my mother. I know it was you."

"She was a great asset, kid. We sent her out dozens of times. A fire here, a fire there. Always a cleanup job, and she did them well. Never questioned anything, probably to make sure we didn't find out about you," Hendricks said. "Shame she didn't open that last package. You left me no choice."

"She was dying!" Henry screamed. "Because of what your people did to her! Because of your damn experiments!"

"You should be thanking me, then. My way was quicker than

what she was going through. Merciful, in a sense."

Flames sparked along the kid's hands and up his arms. "Is that what you call it?"

"No, I personally call it a job well done," Hendricks said. He grinned and raised his pistol. "Like this."

"What happened to coming in?" Henry asked. The fire waned along his skin.

"That was when I could have used you as an asset. Now you're a liability. Shur-Rite brought too much attention, and you didn't move fast enough. It was bound to happen. Promethean has always been a failure of a project." He cocked the hammer back. "Nothing left to do now but sweep up the mess. Your buddies back there too."

Hendricks crooked his head as the rear guard closed in on the nurse's station. Henry was sweating, building on the agent's excitement at the closure to come.

"You said you'd let them go," Henry said.

"After the headache those jackasses caused me?"

"You son of a—"

The bullet erupted from the chamber, Henry's forehead locked in the sight. The projectile zoomed down the hall, blazing for the target, but then, without warning, it shattered before reaching the mark.

"What the hell?" It hit Hendricks in an instant; the heat in the corridor caused sweat to pool along his palms. "How are you still—?"

"Standing?" Henry said with a smirk. "I've been doing a lot of reading lately. Do you know the temperature necessary to ignite the casing of a bullet before impact? I do."

Hendricks growled, jaw tight and pistol poised to fire. He signaled the other men, who converged on the central station and the trio hiding behind the thin barrier.

"I've read the files on your mother, Henry. You don't have enough juice left after everything you've done the last few days. Especially with your new buddies so close to your position."

"What buddies?"

Hendricks' eyes went wide. Realization flooded in as the rear guard loomed over the station, only to find nothing within. It had all been a distraction. Their entire discussion had served as nothing more than a diversion to give Riley and his cohorts precious seconds to escape.

Henry's hands ignited, the flames spreading over his entire body. It burned bright and blinded the wetwork team that had been prepared for little more than the emergency lighting of the abandoned hospital wing. Through the blistering heat and spreading fire, Hendricks witnessed the true power of Henry Reed as it reached the pile of oxygen tanks scattered throughout the wing.

"Oh, sh—"

Then his world exploded.

CHAPTER THIRTY

Zac hated the plan. Inaudible screams clamored in his head at both Ben and Morgan as they fled the second-floor maternity ward. The agents prodded him ever forward, unable to hesitate, unable to think things through.

Thinking was all Zac *could* do anymore. He thought about his arrival in Chicago, about the case at hand and how quickly it had become complicated. He thought about too many things, items on an endless checklist never to be ticked off. Everything centered on Henry Reed and the fight they had left for him to face alone.

"Which way?" Ben whispered. Their staggered steps carried them from the hole melted through the floor above them to the darkened emergency ward below. Morgan ran ahead, hand tight to her grazed shoulder. Zac's pace slowed as the tablet screen lit up before him.

He offered no response to the question, though he scanned the diagram centered on the display for an answer. His glassy eyes were lost on the argument above. He had failed to come up with a solution to save them all, his silence forcing the others to pick up his slack. He was out of his element and had been the entire time. He wasn't meant for field work—for anything, really. His life, complete with expectations and responsibilities, called to him, yet he held no answers.

"Zac?"

Zac shook his head, flipping the diagram around for a better look.

"Down here," Morgan called as she waved them on.

Ben pushed the hesitant tech ahead. Zac ran headlong into a

waiting tray of equipment, left in the center of the hall as an afterthought. It spilled before him, Ben's hand tight to his collar to keep him standing—to keep him moving away from the shouting growing from the gaping hole above.

He stopped at the end of the wing, the doors to the hall covered in plywood. From the opposite side, Ben slammed at the glass separating them from what had been the main lobby. Morgan tore at the corners of a plank of wood covering the emergency exit.

Zac did nothing—the same as always. He was useless, lost to the fight and unable to see a way out. He wished he was brave like the man they'd left behind. He wished he could be something more.

"How much time do we have?"

Ben joined Morgan and the two ripped the wood loose from the door. "Not enough for a conversation."

"We shouldn't have left him," Zac said. It was a lesson they had learned time and time again, yet they continued to fail at it when it came to their work. Grissom. Ruth. Now Henry. When would it be enough? When would the sacrifice be enough?

Ben shuffled the debris out of the way as Morgan kicked at the latch on the door. The emergency exit snapped open. The night air rushed in and the parking lot extended before them.

Their freedom was finally within reach.

"You know I'm right, Morgan," Zac continued, unable to keep from glancing at the hole in the ceiling down the hall—unable to leave Henry to his fate.

Her hand fell on his arm. "Keep moving, Zac."

He stood his ground. "We can't leave him like this."

"He's doing this for us," Ben replied. He offered a sad smile, understanding in his eyes. "Let's not disappoint him."

There was no more time. No more arguing. The choice had been made and they had to live with the decision. Zac hoped Henry would be able to do the same.

"We need to move!" Morgan snapped from the door. "Now."

Zac nodded and rushed for the outside air. Ben followed close. Morgan led them farther through the parking lot and away from Edgewater Medical Center. Gunfire erupted above. Screams echoed along the shattered windows of the second floor.

"Henry—"

Ben grabbed him and pulled him along the pavement. "Not safe yet, buddy. Come on."

"We're not?" Zac asked, the cold stinging his lungs. "Riley, what are you—?"

The initial shockwave of the explosion sent both men soaring across the parking lot. They crashed hard against the ground. They slid along the slick pavement and came to a halt at Morgan's crouched form. Her hands covered her ears, and her eyes were closed to the raining glass blasted loose along the entire second floor of the facility.

Flames sparked throughout the building. Smoke rose in plumes against the night sky and blotted out the Chicago skyline.

Zac struggled for breath. He fought for his knees. Ben kept him close, both coughing from the impact. All three fell silent, lost to the flames consuming the abandoned hospital.

"Henry..."

CHAPTER THIRTY-ONE

Smoke drifted along the parking lot, wafting up into the night sky before it dissipated against the darkness. The fire faded, the diligent work of emergency crews rushing back and forth along the edifice of the long-forgotten structure.

Flashing lights filled the parking lot. Local police surveyed the wreckage where they could. Fire and rescue cleared the medical center wing by wing before access was granted to forensics. Eventually, the FBI turned up, hoping for information on the entire affair, and to cast blame where they saw fit.

"Let me see if I have this straight," Section Chief Hannah Wilcox bellowed at the quiet pair of DSA agents. She had found them immediately upon arriving. "This guy flashes a badge and you take him at his word? No confirmation from our office or your own?"

Wilcox wasn't wrong. Their pursuit of Henry had clouded the entire case, the trust displayed in Hendricks more out of necessity than anything else, yet it had played right into the traitor's hands.

"When you put it that way it does sound a good bit worse than the reality of the situation," Ben said, attempting to appease the scarlet-haired agent. It failed on every level. Her cold eyes drove him behind Morgan in defeat.

"I ran his ID," Morgan started. "Agent Hendricks—"

"Is dead," snapped Wilcox. She let out a long breath, hands to her hips. Her voice softened in reflection. "He has been for days, from what the assistant M.E. is telling me. We found him in the trunk."

All turned to Hendricks' car on the far side of the lot. A pair of investigators pored over the interior, while another rummaged through the trunk for answers.

"Then Hendricks wasn't—"

"Who the hell was he?" Morgan finished.

Wilcox continued, the remnants of the blaze reflected within her thin blue eyes. "We've been looking ever since he failed to report in two days ago. We coordinated the case with local authorities while wondering why our friends at the DSA weren't responding through proper channels."

"We were—" Morgan stopped. Every contact had been offered by Hendricks. Their reports, their every status update, were intercepted by his people.

"Instead," Wilcox continued, "you've been running around blowing up buildings in my city."

"This one was abandoned, at least," Ben clarified.

Morgan shook her head, blocking him from Wilcox's full wrath. "Ma'am, you'll find that the men inside were responsible for Reginald Kane's death as well as Anna Reed. They set the fire here."

The glower from Wilcox turned to Morgan. "Convenient that they're all dead, isn't it."

"Faulty equipment, I'd say," Ben interjected before dropping back once more.

"I'll wait for the report from my own people, Agent Riley. If that's all right with you, that is?"

"Sounds fair."

The frustrated official sighed. "I would be open to an explanation as to how they decided an abandoned hospital suited their needs as a target? Or how you two yutzes stumbled upon them?"

"All great questions."

Morgan rolled her eyes. "What my partner is trying to say is—"

"Partner?!" Ben exclaimed.

"Don't let it go to your head," chided Morgan.

"Too late," Ben replied with a toothy grin. Wilcox's arms crossed her chest, aggravation burning hotter than the waning flames from the hospital. "Sorry. We're having a moment here."

He moved in for a hug and Morgan held him back. "We were."

"It's gone now, isn't it?"

Her smile beamed. All the anger and the frustration melted away, turning into the genuine first step to something new between the two of them—something hopeful and real.

Wilcox fought to keep her cool. Her nails dug into her forearms. "No, please continue," she grumbled. "I don't have anything else to do tonight. What with the three dead guys and the complete lack of answers."

"Wait," Ben stopped. "Three?"

"Welcome back to the actual conversation."

Ben pushed through, eyes locked on the burnt husk that had once been the second floor of the medical center. "You mean to say there were four bodies, don't you?"

"No," Wilcox replied. "I'm pretty sure my team can count, especially when it comes to the well-done remains of tonight's barbecue."

"You don't think—"

"Hendricks," Ben whispered. There was no doubt which of the four would have been lucky enough to escape the blast. "Or whoever the hell he was."

"How did he survive that?" Morgan asked.

Ben turned away from the smoldering ashes of the evening, scanning the silent streets and waiting to catch sight of the mystery man. "Remind me to ask him the next time I see him."

The pair fell silent. The unending lecture from Wilcox carried them into the next hour. Reasoning failed their argument, but she begrudgingly accepted their account of events. Hendricks— the false one—had given them an excuse for skirting natural protocols.

Eventually the yelling subsided. Wilcox returned to her team, the demands of the investigation pulling her back. Ben was grateful for the reprieve and the peace of the night. Their car waited, the window still shattered and the passenger looking out, covered in a blanket offered by the emergency crews.

His presence still remained one of the many mysteries to the affair. Ben let it drop, not caring any longer. Zac had been through enough.

"Everything good?" Morgan asked. Her hand fell on the sill, grazing Zac's fingers.

He smiled and nodded. She patted his hand.

Zac turned away. "How about you?"

All eyes fell on the passenger side and the dust-covered face of Henry Reed. He huddled his naked body beneath a second blanket.

Ben had gone back for him after the blast. While flames sparked up and down the second floor wing, the nervous agent had refused to wait any longer to retrieve a man willing to sacrifice so much for a group of strangers that had cost him more than they cared to admit. Ben had found the man waiting at the nurse's station, the fire retreating from him with each step as he attempted to climb down to the emergency ward.

Henry rested along the seat. "Ask me again tomorrow."

"Fair enough," Ben admitted.

"You two?"

The pair shared a silent glance, both unable to keep from looking back at the hospital and the unanswered questions lost within.

Morgan shook her head. "Not by a long shot."

"Par for the course around here," Ben said. He reached for the door handle. "Want me to—?"

Morgan smiled. "I've got it, partner. I've got it."

CHAPTER THIRTY-TWO

Their flight home was quick, the group silent and resting the entire way. Metcalf had met them at Dulles, escorting Ben and Morgan personally while security offered Zac and Henry their own transport.

Lectures aside, the conversation remained tepid. The debriefing was thorough from both agents. Metcalf fought back a selection of curses, but at the end of things she thanked them for their work.

The sun wavered along the morning sky. It struggled to push through the gray clouds shifting in their direction. Ben left the DSA warehouse for home. Since he was tired, both mentally and physically, little dissuaded him from a night of cartoon violence and sack time.

Then the gray sedan appeared.

He caught sight of it in the mirror of the cab. A stray glance and there it sat, three cars back and one lane over. Two men sat within, their eyes locked on his bumper as if the cab might suddenly disappear.

"Change of plans," he muttered to the driver. "I feel like doing some shopping."

He passed along a twenty with the instructions, his intention clear. The cabbie skirted out of traffic at the earliest intersection and started for the Westfield Montgomery Mall. Impulsive and dangerous, but it was the only move left to him.

His surveillance refused to fall back, refused to take the hint, and continued their task. Eventually they would tire, but what that would mean for his options frightened him more than his current course of action.

Tamara grinned at his arrival, and worked to mix his usual smoothie. He thanked her, though her story about her week fell on deaf ears. Money slid across the counter, more than he'd meant to leave. He was too distracted to argue the point and she never said a word about the exchange.

Ben took a seat at his usual table. He placed his phone next to his drink, reading the clock as he scanned the food court. All exits were covered. Even his typical radius was shrinking as an uncomfortably silent middle-aged couple edged closer to his position to eavesdrop.

He didn't give them a chance to settle, jumping to his feet and starting for the restroom. The clock ticked off another minute, and his heart raced. Short bursts of communication shuffled between wandering eyes around the room. Three groups were on the outskirts, checking in with the others for updates. Those closer to the action waited, likely not wanting to expose their position without warrant, though to Ben they had in their momentary panic over his sudden departure.

His pace quickened and he shuffled through the stragglers meandering along the lengthy hall leading to the restrooms. Near the ladies room, Ben halted. He leaned against the wall, while his foot tapped away the seconds on the clock.

When she exited the family washroom, Ben started walking again. The mother with the stroller struggled to make the sharp turn back to the mall, and when the door closed Ben collided with her.

The stroller halted, its contents secured. The woman's purse, however, soared loose from her arm. Items scattered across the corridor.

Ben crouched to collect the goods. "I'm so sorry, miss. Let me help you with that."

"It's fine," the startled woman replied. She joined him in shuffling receipts and keys into the waiting bag. "I can—"

"No trouble at all," Ben said. His full hands passed along the remaining items. "Again, I'm sorry about this."

"Th... thank..." the mother stuttered, laboring to sling her purse over her arm. Ben guided her back to the waiting stroller. "Thank you..."

"Have a good day!" Ben waved. "Sorry again."

Without a second glance, though plenty were thrown his way

by the worried woman, Ben ducked into the men's room. He locked the door and ducked into the closest stall. The mother's cell phone slipped loose from his sleeve.

Dialing quickly, Ben huddled close and listened impatiently to the ringing. Three full chimes echoed in the empty space before the line clicked over.

"Flint here," the desk sergeant at his old precinct answered. "How can I—?"

Ben cleared his throat, lowering his voice. "Emily Wright there?"

"Wright?"

"Yeah," Ben grumbled through the receiver. "Sergeant Emily Wright."

She was the only person he trusted. Sure, a bond had formed with Morgan over the course of their time in Chicago, one he hoped would build to something given time and patience. Those, however, were two elements no longer in supply when it came to the surveillance monitoring his every move.

He needed to solve what had happened to him in Buffalo—to learn the truth behind the frame job that had taken his life from him. There was no choice in his eyes but to reach outside the DSA, to reconnect with the only person willing to stand with him through everything back home. Emily was more than just a partner: she was the one connection he refused to sever.

He needed her help.

Flint returned to the line. "Ain't no one by that name here. Not anymore."

The phone fell away from his ear and almost dropped into the open toilet. Flint's voice called out through the line twice, waiting for a response.

Instead, Ben ended the call. Emily lived for her job. It fulfilled her on a level it never had for him. She made the work a lifestyle, one she fought for every day that culminated in her promotion to Sergeant.

Another call chimed, her house number dialed this time. Time slipped away. His keepers were no doubt working their way slowly to his position.

The phone rang once before clicking over.

"Emily?" Ben said. "Oh, thank—"

"Hang up right now, Agent Riley," a voice boomed in his ear.

It was garbled, as if synthesized through a computer program.

"What?" Ben staggered, rechecking the number. "Who is this? What's happened to Emily Wright?"

"Let her go, Agent Riley. Final warning."

The phone went dead. With it, his last hope fell away. Ben shambled from the stall for the sink. Setting the phone next to him, he cupped his hands and filled them with water from the faucet. After splashing the cool liquid over his face, Ben let it stream down his cheeks.

The lock turned over and he started back to the food court. A pair of out-of-place men in suits moved for his location, still shuffling through the crowds in the food court at the end of the hall. Ben paused, unsure where to go, what to do, when the door to the women's room opened.

The mother with the stroller had returned, cutting off his view of the two suited agents. Her eyes widened at the sight of him. "Hey," she called. "Have you seen—?"

Ben handed her the phone. "It must have slipped under the door."

"Thank you," she exclaimed.

"Not a problem." Ben never looked in her direction, eyes locked instead on the peering faces from the crowd at the end of the hall.

A hand hooked along his arm, halting him. The mother smiled and leaned close, her voice little more than a whisper. "You're not safe, Agent Riley. Your choices will only put you in danger. As well as those you care about."

"What?" he asked, fighting for words. The men continued to approach, their steps a bit more cautious with the arrival of the woman and the stroller. "How do you know—?"

"They monitored your first call," she continued. "I had to intervene."

"That was you? What happened to Emily?"

"This isn't about her, Agent Riley. But if you continue this path you won't be able to protect her."

"Who are you?" he asked. He struggled to keep his voice down. The inside of the stroller was now visible. Blankets were bunched along the carrier, obscuring the lack of a baby within. "Why am I being followed?"

"For your protection," the woman said. "At least on my end.

As for your friends in the suits and the shoulder holsters? Let's just say there are more players involved than you know. You need to be smart about your next move."

"Which should be?"

"Figuring out the agent you want to be and the job you want to be doing," the woman said with a smile. "Your answers will come. The people that set you up will be brought to light. Right now though? The DSA needs you, Ben. Probably more than you need it.

"Now get out of here," she said, giving a nod to the emergency exit at the end of the corridor. "I'll keep them occupied."

With that, she wheeled her empty stroller for the food court. When the agents were in reach of her, she feigned tripping over the wheel of the stroller. In her stumble, the stroller spun wide and blocked the entire corridor. Ben took the moment to duck out through the exit.

Who was that woman? Did she work for the DSA or someone else entirely?

His trust was in short supply and his options were quickly running out on where to turn. Emily was his one and only connection with his previous life, his last chance to understand what the DSA truly was and how much control they held over his current situation. Instead, the crisis was much worse than he had ever imagined.

They knew about Emily. Because of him, because of his stupidly selfish act of reaching out to her, Ben had put a target on her. She was now in danger and there wasn't a damn thing he could do to help. Ben left the mall behind, breaking into a run for his apartment — afraid of the growing shadows closing in on him from all sides.

CHAPTER THIRTY-THREE

Zac clung tight to his brief bag, his steps slow and steady along the wide entrance hall of the DSA warehouse. Debriefing had taken hours. Questions had come from Stephanie of all people. The secretary had demanded details of an operation Zac never should have been a part of in the first place. He'd let it happen, as he did with much of his life, bending over backward for people in authority rather than standing up to them as equals.

Part of him had hoped Chicago might change things, that new opportunities, new perceptions, were possible after years of endless routine. He was, however, the same old Zac, stuck in a rut of his own making. His frustration mounted, and he reflexively squeezed his hands along the strap of his bag. Leaning along the wall, Zac closed his eyes and tried to wish the thoughts away.

Along with the object of his anger.

"Zac!" Metcalf called. Her flats clicked loudly along the tile toward him. "A moment."

He sighed. His eyes remained clamped shut, hoping her voice rested only in his head. When he finally opened them she was standing across from him in the hall.

"Susan," he muttered. "I'm tired."

"Direc—"

"It's been a week," he continued over her clarification. "I want to squeeze in my standard six hours, maybe say hello to my wife and son without following it with a quick goodbye, before heading back here. I'm sure you understand."

"I do."

Zac huffed, then forced a smile. "You really just don't care."

"I enjoyed your debriefing," Metcalf said, leaning beside him as the hallway cleared of personnel. "Very biting commentary on what happened. I prefer to keep it fact oriented."

"I'll try to remember that," he replied. Irritation crept in his voice. "When I'm not being abducted or shot at by *Splinter Cell* rejects, that is."

"I don't—"

"It's a video game," he said. "You know what? Never mind."

"You're upset."

Zac kicked off the wall. "I mentioned the whole shooting-at-me thing."

"It won't be happening again," Metcalf said. Her words matched her demeanor, cold and calculated.

When Zac had joined there was an edge to her, but her humanity had poked through the surface more often than not. Since Grissom's death, however, Susan Metcalf had grown cold to the world.

There was never a question when it came to her orders, to the way she ran the Department of Special Assignments. Their mandate was clear, their objectives noble. But lately? Doubts crept to the surface, the questions over her leadership too frequent to discount.

"Somehow I doubt that."

"Believe what you will," Metcalf said. She guided him to a quiet corner outside her office. "I still need that report. The *other* report."

"Right." Her concern for his well-being was non-existent. All that mattered was the mission—in this case, the one that had brought him to Chicago in the first place. He had arrived the second Reginald Kane's body turned up, the moment before Morgan had taken up the case as her own. The case was never meant to be for her at all. It had always been meant for Benjamin Riley.

"I need your assessment of Agent Riley."

Zac scoffed, hands to his hips. "My spying on him, you mean."

"Zac."

"He's an ass," the analyst stated. "He's belligerent and frustrating to everyone around him."

"And?"

"And he had our backs the entire operation. He knew Henry was innocent before any of us realized it, but never let it sway our findings. Hell, he probably knew about Hendricks, or whoever the hell that guy was, too."

Through all their arguments, through the bickering between him and Morgan, Ben had stood for what Zac always believed possible at the agency. He fought for a cause while Zac cowered behind red tape and orders. Maybe that was where their animosity had originated: a place of jealousy instead of a true reason. Either way, the Head of Operational Support and Research was glad to have had Ben at his side over the last few days.

"Anything else?" Metcalf asked, reading his thoughts.

"Yeah," he breathed. "Why are you watching him so closely? Resources to follow him on downtime? Now in the field? Why recruit him at all?"

He wasn't meant to know, since the allocation had been done through a workaround. Zac was never without resources of his own, however, and it surprised her for a quick moment before her sharp blue eyes went cold once more.

"I can't answer that."

"I figured as much."

Her hand fell on his shoulder, patting lightly. "Get some rest."

Metcalf started for the open door to her office. Zac called after her. "What about Henry?"

"Mr. Reed?"

"I was hoping to see him before he left."

"He's fine."

"Free and clear?" Zac pressed.

"Zac…"

"Where, then?" Frustration crested and he fought to rein it in. "Where is he?"

"Containment protocol."

"The Ark? Why?"

Her lips pursed. "He burned a man to death when he was threatened. He set fire to a hospital—abandoned, yes, but next time? I had no choice in this, Zac." She read his disapproval. "Henry's somewhere capable of helping him learn to control his ability. It's for the best."

He understood it. Disliked it, for sure, but he understood the reason behind the decision—especially if the disease that had slowly killed his mother might someday affect Henry in the same manner. Better the young man be surrounded with care than out in the world on his own.

Or so Zac justified the choice. "You'll check in on him?"

"Of course."

"Good," Zac said. He tucked his bag close and started down the hall. His wife and son waited for him. The promise of a few hours of sleep soothed his troubled spirit. His last words to Metcalf echoed behind him. "After the mess he went through, Henry Reed deserves a little peace. We all do."

CHAPTER THIRTY-FOUR

Doctor Wyatt Jensen waited patiently on the heli-pad. He stood in the center of his organization's emblem: the image of a man sitting beneath an apple tree lost to his shadow. The oil rig rarely welcomed air traffic to the refurbished facility. When the helicopter arrived, wind ripped through him and threatened to launch him to the waves below.

The military-issued transport shimmered in the moonlight surrounding their location off the Gulf Coast. Two men in lab coats stood behind him, and his nerves rose with each rotation of the propeller. Every new arrival to the facility was a lesson, each threatening the secrecy of the location.

As the spinning blades of the copter came to a halt, the two men approached quickly. The back door opened and they jumped into the transport. From the opposite side, a single individual wearing a thick sweater vest and dark brown khakis stepped on the platform. Moonlight shone off his smile.

"Welcome back, sir," Jensen said.

"Have all the arrangements been made?" the man asked, moving for the main structure. The lab techs returned to the platform, the contents from the copter between them. A stasis tube. Thick wheels shook loose from beneath, extending to the platform like a medical bed. Jensen nodded to his employer, then ushered them forward toward the double doors under a slight alcove that led deeper into the structure.

"This way. Yes," Jensen said. His pace slowed to avoid running into his own crew. Though he had earned the role of lead scientist, every instinct made him inferior. Every interaction left him full of guilt and *what-if* scenarios, and they occupied his every thought. He buried them as deep as the drill at the center of the rig — or tried to at least — whenever management came for a visit. "Asset Control has been waiting for your arrival."

"And the other station?"

Jensen nodded once again, unable to look the man in the face. Something in his smile unnerved the scientist. "Documents are being falsified as we speak. Everything will appear legitimate for Director Metcalf."

"On paper."

"Yes," Jensen continued as the team entered the alcove off the heli-pad. A lift carried them to the lower levels. When it reached the end, a small barrier opened to the entrance of the facility. At the end of the hall was a pair of doors and a single keypad. Jensen took the lead, calling back to his employer, who followed briskly with the lab techs and their precious cargo in the rear. "The Florida institute remains in the dark. Any inquiries about our patient here will route directly to us."

Jensen typed in his access code. The man in the vest read the label above the doors with pride, the same way he did every visit.

THE ARK

"Poor Susan," the man said. The doors opened before him. Jensen took up position beside the elder statesman. "Always relying on paperwork to see the world when the reality of the situation has to be seen to be believed. Isn't that right, Mr. Reed?"

If the young man in the stasis tube could have answered, his response would have been filled with a few words on the colorful side of the English language. Fortunately for Jensen and his team, all words and all consciousness escaped the new ward of the Ark as the techs pushed him deeper through the structure. It had been a simple matter to redirect Henry's transport away from the institute portion of the Ark, the public face that Metcalf knew about. Especially when the man in charge of making the transfer arrangements stood proudly in front of the double doors.

Deputy Director Greg Sullivan.

He followed the techs and their new subject through the labyrinth of corridors that stretched in all directions around the expansive rig. Each hall entered into a specialized division. Xeno-biology. Genetic engineering. Retroviruses. Inhuman. Meta-human. Subhuman. The Ark was a treasure trove of oddities and miracles found around the planet.

Sullivan's stride carried him past the techs pushing the heavy stasis tube. He led them left, down a winding hall to another set of doors, labeled in deep red above.

ASSET CONTROL

"Put him on ice. Same as the others," Sullivan said as the doors opened. He nodded to the techs, the two silent observers taking Henry into the ward. Sullivan stopped Jensen before he could follow. "Has there been any word?"

"We haven't heard from the operative sent to handle the situation in Chicago."

"I'm afraid I put too much stock in his abilities when I brought him into this." A sly grin curled at the end of his lips. "Even in his failure to quietly remove Kane from the board, Henry Reed has given us more than we bargained for: an excuse to appease the Trust's interest and a tool for the future of our work."

Sullivan was already within the ward when Jensen caught up to him. They were surrounded by dozens of occupied tubes on a large platform that ran down the center of the row. Coolant escaped around them, billowing up Jensen's lab coat, and it almost knocked over the waif of a man.

The techs tipped the stasis tube upright. Once properly aligned, they connected the tube to the larger network within. Henry never flinched, caught in an unending sleep that matched the other members of the wing, all deeply dreaming in a cryogenic freeze.

"Monitor him closely."

"Of… of course, sir," Jensen stammered. "It's just—"

"Just what, Jensen?" Sullivan asked, clearly proud of the completed operation in front of them.

"The variables involved here," Jensen started, his voice low and filled with concern. "The manpower required to keep the subjects contained. What I'm trying to say is… Why bother keeping any of them?"

"A fair question, Jensen. And a simple answer," Sullivan said. He turned to Henry's neighbor, another recent recruit to the Ark. His hand grazed the front of the apparatus, wiping away the condensation collected around the nameplate on the face of the tube. Etched in bold letters was a name.

JACOB GRISSOM

"You never know when an asset might be needed."

ABOUT THE AUTHOR

Lou Paduano is the author of the Greystone series of urban fantasy adventures, which follow Detective Greg Loren and Soriya Greystone as they hunt myths, monsters, and legends in the city of Portents.

He is also the author of the conspiracy thriller series, The DSA, a serialized tale about a clandestine government agency trying to discover the true power behind humanity's future.

He lives in Grand Island, New York with his wife and three daughters. Sign up for his e-mail list for free content as well as updates on future releases at loupaduano.com.

THE GREYSTONE SAGA

AVAILABLE NOW

Follow the adventures of Soriya Greystone and Detective Greg Loren as they hunt dangerous myths and legends in the city of Portents.

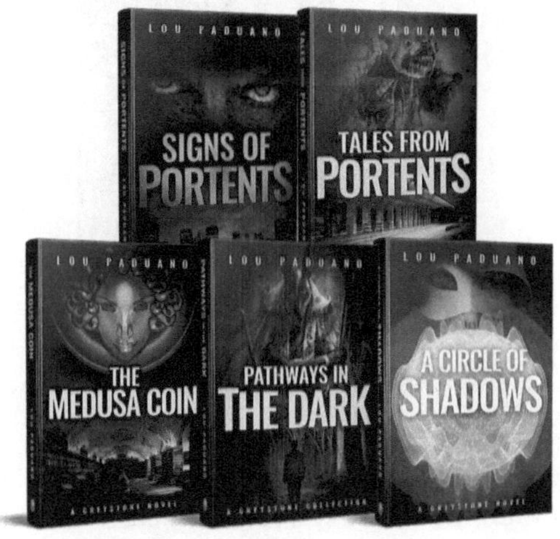

BOOK ONE - SIGNS OF PORTENTS
BOOK TWO - TALES FROM PORTENTS
BOOK THREE - THE MEDUSA COIN
BOOK FOUR - PATHWAYS IN THE DARK
BOOK FIVE - A CIRCLE OF SHADOWS

ALSO AVAILABLE NOW

It's her first case and it might be her last.

Soriya has worked her entire life to become the Greystone —
protector of her city, Portents, against the growing shadows of
myth and legend. All her efforts are in jeopardy when she is
struck down by the destructive power of the Minotaur.

Soriya must now find a new path. Only one thing is certain —
she's going to need help.

The secrets of Soriya's training are revealed in the first adven-
ture of this new Greystone trilogy!

THE MYSTERY BEGINS

The residents of Bellbrook, Ohio have vanished.

Seven thousand people in a four-mile radius disappeared overnight. A dead zone remains, no outgoing signals emanating from the ghost town.

Ben Riley, framed for a crime he never committed, is the latest recruit to the Department of Special Assignments — a secret agency handling unsolved cases, those with open questions and unexplainable circumstances. Unsure what to expect or whether or not he deserves this second chance, Ben is thrust into a bizarre case of science gone wrong.

Now, Ben and the rest of the field team must find out what happened to the residents of Bellbrook… before it happens to them.

THE DSA CONTINUES IN…

A sniper's bullet changed Lincoln MacKenzie's life forever.

Lincoln has been tasked with a mission: to hunt down the Witness — the enigmatic man behind the tragedy in Bellbrook. Present and past entwine as Lincoln is forced to make a choice between ending the life of the Witness or saving him from a far more dangerous threat.

Will Lincoln's desire for revenge outweigh his need for the truth?

Meanwhile, Ben Riley is caught in the middle of a political game as his assessment begins before the Inter-Agency Council. But is the purpose behind his questioning only the opening gambit of a larger plot against not only the Director of the DSA, but the agency itself?

www.ingramcontent.com/pod-product-compliance
Lightning Source LLC
Chambersburg PA
CBHW032027180726
48284CB00008B/2507